CHRIS PLATT

Ω
PEACHTREE
ATLANTA

Ω

Published by
PEACHTREE PUBLISHERS
1700 Chattahoochee Avenue
Atlanta, Georgia 30318-2112
www.peachtree-online.com

Cover design by Loraine M. Joyner and Maureen Withee
Book design by Melanie McMahon Ives

Printed in July 2010 by Lake Book Manufacturing in Melrose Park, Illinois, in the United States of America
10 9 8 7 6 5 4 3 2 1
First Edition

Library of Congress Cataloging-in-Publication Data

Platt, Chris, 1959-
  Astra / written by Chris Platt.
      p. cm.
   Summary: Forbidden to ride after her mother's death in a riding accident, thirteen-year-old Lily nurses her mother's beloved horse, Astra, back to health, hoping that someday Astra will win the Tevis Cup endurance race.
   ISBN 978-1-56145-541-6 / 1-56145-541-5
   [1. Endurance riding (Horsemanship)–Fiction. 2. Horses–Training–Fiction. 3. Arabian horse–Fiction. 4. Fathers and daughters–Fiction.] I. Title.
   PZ7.P7123115Ast 2010
   [Fic]–dc22
                              2010001654

To all the endurance riders who have done thousands of miles in the saddle, and seen some of the most beautiful wilderness God has to offer. I am honored to have ridden my share of miles with you.

A very special thanks to AERC competitors
Jerry Zebrack and Joyce Stoffey.
You're awesome and you taught me a lot.
Thanks also to endurance rider Patti Mehserle
for all the ride and regulation information,
along with some good stories.

One

ate again! Thirteen-year-old Lily O'Neil rolled out of bed and reached for her jeans, shivering as the cold air touched her skin. Her breath frosted the air as she pulled a sweatshirt over her head and slipped on her boots. The pot-bellied stove must have gone out during the night. It was late February in her small northern California town, and winter promised more cold weather to come.

She rubbed the frost off the inside of her window and peered through the early morning light to the house and stable next door. Whispering Pines Ranch, with its large white house and huge twenty-stall barn nestled at the base of the beautiful Sierra Nevada foothills, was a sight to behold.

Lily looked at the chipped paint on her windowsill and sighed. She loved the quaint little farmhouse she shared with her father and grandma, but the barn at Whispering Pines was bigger than their house and small stable put together.

The owner of Whispering Pines, Steven Henley, raised Arabian endurance horses and competed successfully on a national level. Lily hoped to someday follow in her mother's footsteps and ride for Mr. Henley. One of his best mares, Astra Atomica, was a favorite of Lily's and had the potential to become a champion like her half sister, Contina. Lily desperately wanted to see Astra become a great endurance horse.

The problem was, after the accident, Lily's overprotective father had forbidden her to ever ride again. He didn't even want her *around* horses. She'd never get a chance to step into Astra's saddle.

She thought about Domino, the beautiful black and white pony she'd been forced to sell. Her mother would have hated that idea.

Luckily her grandmother had been on her side. Grams had convinced Lily's father to let her help groom and feed the horses in Mr. Henley's stable. If her father had his way, Lily would never set eyes on another horse again. But horses were her life, just like they'd been for her mom. And right now she didn't want to think about any of this anymore.

Lily ran out her bedroom door and bounded down the stairs two at a time. She crossed the living room on the way to their small, cozy kitchen, and spied her grandmother stoking the potbellied stove. "Here, Grams, let me do that," Lily said. She took the pieces of wood from her grandmother's weathered hands and fed them into the fire.

"Thank you, dear," Grams said, dusting the tree bark off her hands. "Your father was so tired when he went to bed last night, I think he forgot to stock the stove." She pulled her sweater close about her shoulders and shivered.

Tossing the last log on the fire, Lily closed the stove door. Her father had been working a lot of overtime lately. It didn't surprise her that he'd been dead-dog tired at the end of the day. She suspected the family was behind on their bills and he was putting in extra hours to make up for it. Things had been pretty tough lately.

"I made you a nice cup of hot tea and some toast," Grams said. "I know you won't take the time to sit down to a full meal when there are horses to be fed and cared for next door," she added with a wink.

Lily grabbed her hat and jacket off the hook by the back door, then picked up the toast, stuffing half a piece into her mouth. She chased it down with tea so hot it almost burned her mouth.

"Thanks, Grams." Lily wiped the crumbs off her lips and gave her grandmother a peck on the cheek. "I'll be home in a few hours. Hopefully, Dad will sleep in a bit today. He's working too hard." She zipped up her jacket and headed out the door.

Lily's bicycle stood propped against the side of the house. She got on and pedaled down the dirt road that ran in front of the two houses, turning down the long dirt driveway that led to Whispering Pines.

Along the way, she passed white-fenced paddocks filled with beautiful Arabian horses. Lily always marveled at their long, elegant necks and perfectly shaped heads. Several of the horses looked up at the sound of her bike and cocked their tails over their backs, racing down the fence line toward the barn.

Grace and elegance on four legs, her mother used to call the spirited beauties. A deep sadness crept over Lily at the thought of her mom, and she pushed it away. *One day at a time,* she reminded herself.

The front tire of her bike dropped into a pothole, splattering muddy water on her pant legs. Lily's teeth clacked together and she almost lost control of the bike. She quickly realized she'd better take her eyes off the horses and pay attention to the road.

She pedaled into the barnyard and parked her bike under the tall ponderosa pines. More memories washed over her. She thought about the times she rode Domino over to join her mother for the long walk down the dirt road on one of the racers. Mr. Henley required the walk to loosen up the horses for their upcoming workouts.

Lily had loved making that ride with her mother, rocking to the rhythmic swing of Dominic's stride. Back then, she'd imagined the day she'd get to ride one of the awesome Arabian racers.

Sometimes her mom let her trot the first mile or two of the workout. But Domino would soon tire and want to head back to the barn. The racer always picked up the pace and headed up the mountain trail with ears pricked and tail floating on the wind. Lily had watched them go, vowing that someday she'd follow in her mom's boot steps and become a great endurance rider herself. *Yeah, right!* Lily scoffed at herself now. Domino had managed to dump her on her backside on a regular basis, and he was fairly well broke. The high-spirited Arabians with their catlike reflexes would guarantee her almost as much time on the ground as she'd spend in the saddle. But she was determined to become a better rider— just as soon as her father allowed her to ride again. And that would probably be never.

"Good morning, Lily." Mr. Henley straightened his tall, thin frame and eyed his watch. "You're a bit late this morning."

"I'm sorry, Mr. Henley." Lily shoved her hands deep into her pockets and looked at the ground. "I, uh…overslept."

Mr. Henley could be super strict sometimes. Lily hoped her tardiness wouldn't be cause for him to let her go. Her father allowed her to help Mr. Henley with the horses partly because he was their neighbor. But if Mr. Henley didn't want

4

her to help anymore, she'd be out of luck. Her father wasn't likely to let her care for anybody else's horses.

Jill, Mr. Henley's sixteen-year-old daughter, handed Lily three grain buckets and pointed her toward the first several stalls. "Dad!" she scolded her father. "Give Lily a break. She comes over here out of the goodness of her heart to help us. It's not like she's an employee." She rolled her eyes and went back to mixing grain.

Lily smiled her thanks at the older girl. Jill had always been nice to her. If they'd been closer in age, they might have been really good friends.

Nickers of excitement echoed up and down the shed row as horses bobbed their heads and pawed the shavings under their hooves in anticipation of breakfast.

Lily quickly fed the horses nearest the tack room, then slipped into Astra's stall. She greeted the beautiful gray Arabian with a good scratch under her mane.

Astra Atomica was the perfect example of an Arabian horse. She had a broad forehead with wide-set, intelligent eyes. Her small curved ears and perfectly dished face led to a petite muzzle with large nostrils. She stood fifteen hands tall—a hand being four inches—and she had well-balanced shoulders and hindquarters.

Lily knew that the success of careful breeding programs over thousands of years meant that today's Arabian was virtually the same horse as the ones ridden in ancient Arabia. They were the oldest known breed of riding horse, and one of the most popular in modern times. And someday she was going to own one!

Astra poked her whiskered muzzle into Lily's pockets, searching for the treat she knew Lily would bring her.

"Here you go, pretty." Lily fed the mare the oats and

molasses horse treats she'd bought with her weekly allowance. While Astra munched happily, Lily poured grain into her feed tub and stepped back to watch the daily ritual. The gray mare stepped forward and stuck her nose deep into the feeder, then swished her head from side to side, pushing the grain around the way a person stirred a bowl. She pawed several times with her right front leg and blew through her lips, then settled in to eat.

"You're so goofy!" Lily said, running her hand lovingly down the mare's long, perfectly arched neck. She laid her cheek against Astra's mane and breathed in the warm horse scent. She knew why her mother had loved this horse. Lily loved her, too. And just like her mother, she also believed that Astra Atomica could place in the Top Ten of the Tevis Cup some day. It had been her mother's dream.

And now it was Lily's.

But unfortunately, she didn't own Astra. She had no control over what happened with her. Mr. Henley wasn't exactly encouraging about the mare's abilities. He had several other big-talent horses in his stable and he poured most of his efforts into them. He saw Astra as just another horse in his stable. She was a safe mare to ride, so he'd given her to his son Charlie to exercise and prepare for the lesser fifty-mile endurance races.

Lily cringed when she thought about Charlie. He was in her grade at school and she had the questionable honor of sitting next to him in math class. Math was bad enough without adding Charlie to the mix. Too bad he couldn't be more like his older sister, Jill.

Charlie was just plain mean. And although he was a good rider—much better than she was—he didn't care much about anyone or anything but himself.

Even worse, he loved to tease Lily.

She pushed Charlie from her thoughts and turned her attention back to Astra. Giving the mare one last pat, she went to help Jill finish the rest of the feeding.

There was a set routine around the barn. Mr. Henley liked doing things a certain way. And since he owned the place, he got exactly what he wanted.

All of the horses were grained first thing in the morning. Racers got the largest portions because they expended the most energy. Broodmares, yearlings, and two-year-olds got the next biggest ration because they were growing or reproducing. Mr. Henley kept the grain supply down on the saddle horses and those being broke to saddle because he didn't want them hyped up and bucking people off.

Once the grain was distributed, the horses were left alone to eat their morning oats and given a few extra minutes to digest. Then the grooms would arrive to pull the racers scheduled for a workout from their stalls. The horses would be brushed and have their hooves picked before being saddled for the exercise riders.

The racers usually stayed out for at least two to three hours, sometimes as long as five or six. While the riders had the horses out on the trail, Lily helped clean their stalls, scrub water buckets, and hang hay nets. Sometimes she even got to move horses from their stalls to the turnout pens.

Lily checked her watch. She had ten minutes until it was time to groom the racers for their morning workouts. She returned the empty grain buckets to the feed room, then made her way down the aisle to Mr. Henley's trophy wall. She didn't look at it as she entered, but instead, stopped and stood for a moment with her eyes closed. She was happy just to listen to the sounds of the horses rustling around in their stalls and breathe in the wonderful mix of horses and fresh hay.

Finally Lily opened her eyes. She was always amazed at the huge number of ribbons and trophies on the shelves. Everywhere she looked among the awards there were photos of horses and riders snapped during a race or crossing the finish line.

Racers weren't allowed to compete until they were five years of age. By then, their bones were developed enough to withstand the grueling races.

Certificates of Mileage were awarded by the American Endurance Ride Conference, and they had their own special place of honor on the wall. Both horses and riders where awarded this special honor. Riders got their awards at the first two hundred fifty miles, then at five hundred, seven hundred fifty, and one thousand miles. After that it was only every thousand miles. In addition, a medallion was given to the horse every thousand miles.

Mr. Henley had two horses over the five thousand mile threshold, and his current star, Contina, was approaching her three-thousand-mile mark. Astra was eight years old and had yet to earn her one-thousand-mile award. Before her mother started riding the mare, they'd had trouble with the horse having sore feet. But her mom had successfully ridden the horse in ten races. The last few, she'd placed in the top five.

Lily let her eyes wander to the photos of her mother and Astra. She stepped closer to the wall and reached out a shaky hand to touch the last photo. It had been taken at the beginning of the Tevis Cup last year, before the accident.

She allowed herself a brief moment to let the pain come crashing in—but only a moment. It filled her with a hollow ache so deep she thought her knees might give way.

The edges of her vision began to gray and tears welled in her eyes. She quickly pulled her hand away from the photo and willed the tears to stop. Her mother wouldn't want her to cry and carry on. She reminded herself to think of all the wonderful times the two of them had shared—just as her mom had asked her to do.

Lost in her thoughts, Lily didn't hear the footsteps approaching behind her.

"Do you always have to stand there and stare at the wall?"

The nasally voice, sounding more like one of her grandmother's old scratchy records than a teenage boy, immediately set her nerves on edge.

Charlie had found her. "You've done it, like, a gazillion times," he added, reaching out to tweak her hair.

Lily twisted around to glare at him, wishing the force of her stare would knock him clear into the manure pile outside the barn door.

Charlie crossed his arms and glared right back, trying to stare her down. "You know, your mom died because of that horse. People say it wasn't anyone's fault, but if I were you, I wouldn't want anything to do with Astra."

"Let's go, loser." Jill strode down the aisle like a blast of January wind and grabbed her brother by the ear. "Get your skinny butt down to the yearling pens and get those corrals cleaned before I decide to tell Dad what you just said," she threatened. "And when you're finished, you owe Lily a major apology."

Charlie slunk away without a word.

Jill shook her head. "He's a jerk," she told Lily. "Don't pay attention to anything he says."

"Thanks, Jill." Lily turned back to the photo of her mother and Astra. "It wasn't the horse's fault. Really. It wasn't anybody's fault."

"I know." Jill nodded in agreement. "Your mom said so

when they pulled her and the mare out of that crevasse. She begged us not to put Astra down."

"I'm really glad you didn't." Lily smiled at Jill. Sometimes the girl seemed like an older sister to Lily. And since she didn't have any siblings, that helped.

She turned and made her way to the tack room. Astra needed to be saddled. The mare's training was important. Because, just like her mother, Lily still believed Astra could place in the Tevis Cup—in spite of that jerk Charlie training her.

Two

ily walked Astra from her stall and snapped her into the cross ties. She pulled out the rubber currycomb and worked it in a circular motion over the mare's sleek coat. Astra cocked her hind leg and relaxed.

Lily swirled the curry faster and faster over the mare's back and withers, still thinking about what Charlie had said. The kid had a lot of nerve making her feel like she was dishonoring her mother's memory.

Astra flicked her tail and bobbed her head, showing her displeasure at the rough grooming.

"Sorry, girl." Lily softened her touch and slowed her brush strokes. "Charlie just makes me so mad sometimes, I can't think straight."

She switched to a soft body brush and sighed. Deep down, she knew Charlie was right, in a way. It was a little weird for her to hang around the horse that had cost her mother her life. Even Lily didn't understand why she loved Astra so much.

But the accident wasn't Astra's fault. Horse and rider had gone down in a freak accident when part of a single-track trail gave way on a steep mountainside. Because of the remoteness of that section of the trail, it had taken the rescue crew hours to get to them. Lily often wondered if those few hours could have made the difference in saving her mother's life.

She finished the grooming and reached for Charlie's saddle and pad. She placed them high on Astra's withers and pulled them back into place so that all the hairs smoothed into position. It was a trick her mother had taught her.

She wished it were her saddle instead of Charlie's. It would be so awesome to ride the spirited mare through the mountain trails and feel that long, sweeping stride as they covered miles and miles of ground.

She tightened the cinch and frowned. That was one of those wishes that would remain just a dream. Charlie was Astra's exercise rider. Even if the boy did let Lily ride the mare, her father would ground her for life if he found out. What a hopeless cause.

"You look pretty serious."

Lily's best friend, Meloney Hancock, stepped off her gelding, Jasper, and snapped him into the cross ties next to Astra. Lily gave her a welcoming smile. This would be Meloney's first year of racing. She lived half a mile down the road and trained with Mr. Henley.

Lily felt a small flare of envy. What she wouldn't give to own a horse and be out on the trail training with Mr. Henley. She quickly tamped down her jealousy. Meloney was a great friend. She deserved this lucky break.

"Jasper's looking great." Lily offered the bay gelding a treat from her pocket. "The spring rides will be here soon. I think he'll be ready."

"I can't wait!" Meloney said. "It's going to be so much fun." She paused. "I'm sorry, Lily. It's not fair for me to be so excited when you can't go."

Lily shrugged. "It's okay. I'm happy for you. You're going

to have a great time." She ran her fingers through Jasper's forelock, straightening the black strands so they centered on his broad forehead. "Besides, I'll be part of your race crew, if my dad will let me. It'll be my job to make sure you and the horses have food and water during the race. I just won't be out on the trails with you, that's all."

She swallowed hard, forcing the bitter lump of longing down her throat. Maybe someday her father would see how much endurance riding meant to her and let her compete with everyone else.

Charlie poked his head out the tack room door. The powdered sugar from the donut he'd devoured was sprinkled down his shirtfront. "Hey, Lil-Pill, got my horse tacked yet? My dad and Jill are almost ready."

Lily frowned. She hated it when he called her that name.

"Just ignore him," Meloney said in a low voice. "In a way, you're lucky you're not riding with us. I've got to listen to Charlie brag for the next three hours."

"Hi, *Melody*." Charlie brushed the donut crumbs off his shirt and gave her a powdery grin.

Meloney frowned. "You know that's not my name, Charlie. You've known me since third grade." She unsnapped Jasper from the cross ties and checked her saddle girth.

"Oh, yeah," he said. "I forgot. Here, let me hold your horse for you while you get on." He followed her out the barn door.

Lily shook her head. She couldn't quite figure Charlie out. He liked to tease her and Meloney, and she thought that maybe he liked them both. But sometimes he was just nasty and rude.

She gathered Astra, made a last check of the equipment, and led the horse outside to the mounting block to wait for Charlie. It was a perfect day for a winter ride. The sun had been up about an hour and the frost was melting off the fences and the brown winter grass. She could still see her breath on the air and her fingers felt cold. But it would be nice weather for the horses. They wouldn't get too hot during their long workout.

She inhaled deeply, taking in the fresh, clean scent of the tall ponderosa pine trees. She loved living here. Everywhere she looked, for as far as she could see, there were mountains and rolling hills dotted with pines and covered in wild grasses, sagebrush, and manzanita.

"Guess we're out of here, Lily. See you later." Meloney turned her horse and joined Mr. Henley and Jill as they started down the driveway.

"Hey, wait for me." Charlie put his foot in the stirrup and swung onto Astra's back. He gave her a boot with his heels, and the mare tossed her head in mild protest before trotting down the gravel driveway.

"Not on the rocks!" Lily hollered after him. Astra was prone to sore feet. If they wanted to keep her sound for the race season, Charlie needed to keep the mare on soft dirt as much as possible. That's how her mother had kept the horse sound through all those races.

Astra stumbled and took a few short steps. Lily shook her head. Charlie wouldn't listen to anyone. He always did as he pleased. What she didn't understand was why Mr. Henley didn't step in and say something to him. The kid knew better. Her mother had had many talks with him about what it would take to keep Astra sound.

But Mr. H. didn't see any point in pampering the horses. He didn't believe in padding their feet if they were tenderfooted or wrapping their legs with liniment after a hard ride. He had the good fortune to ride a strong, good-legged horse.

Contina never had problems. And Mr. Henley expected the rest of his stock to be just as tough.

When the four riders reached the end of the driveway, Meloney turned in her saddle and waved. Lily sighed, wishing she were going with them. She waved back and turned toward the barn. There were stalls to clean and water buckets to fill. Thomas, the barn manager, would keep her busy until the riders returned.

An hour into her cleaning duties, she heard the familiar sound of her father's old pickup pulling into the stable yard. She leaned her cleaning rake against the wall and went to greet him.

"Hi, Dad." Lily walked to the side door of the rusted-out truck and accepted the thermos of hot chocolate and the peanut butter sandwich he handed out the window.

"Good morning, Flower," her father said with a grin. "Working hard?"

Lily shared a quick laugh with her dad. Her elderly grade-school teacher, Mrs. Smith, could never remember which flower she was named for. After repeatedly going through the list of possibilities—Rose, Petunia, Daisy, Iris—the confused teacher had given up and started calling her Flower. It had become a private joke between Lily and her dad.

She studied her father. When had the gray hair crept into the edges of his dark hair and the worry lines into his face? He looked tired. She knew he'd been working extra hours to pay off some of their bills. Her mother's funeral and the time her father had taken off to mourn and take care of Lily had set them back a bit. But he never complained.

"What's the matter, honey?"

"Nothing." Lily shrugged.

Mr. O'Neil rubbed a calloused hand through his short hair

and frowned. "I know you'd love to be out there on the trails with your friends, kiddo, but I can't let you do it. It's too dangerous, and it's too soon. Maybe in a couple of years I'll reconsider."

Lily bit her lip. She would have liked to be preparing for a race season like the rest of them, of course, but her main concern at the moment was her dad. He looked old and worn out. But she didn't dare say anything. When she'd tried in the past to discuss her fears, he'd told her it was none of her concern.

It *was* her concern, though. Her father probably thought he was protecting her. He didn't understand that shutting her out wasn't helping anything. It just made her worry more.

Her dad started the old truck and put it in gear. "I'm heading to the next valley over for a plumbing job. You be good and help your grandma with dinner. I'll be home by the time it's on the table."

Lily leaned through the truck window and gave her father a peck on the cheek. "Aren't I always good?" she teased.

Her father nodded. "For now, but I'm sure the time's coming." He winked and backed out of the driveway, waving as he sped down the road.

Lily went back to work. Thomas kept her occupied scrubbing water buckets and filling hay nets. Before she knew it, the horses and riders returned.

She could always tell when they were coming down the mountain. It started with a single whinny from one of the horses in a distant field. As the racers got closer, several more neighs of greeting rang out from surrounding pastures. By the time the group reached the one-mile stretch of dirt road leading home, all the pastured horses cantered down the fence line to meet them. Lily could feel the vibration from the hoofbeats as they tore single file down the pasture trail to escort the riders back to the barn.

Finishing the last of the hay nets, Lily went to meet the returning riders. She was surprised to see Charlie walking up the driveway on foot, leading Astra by her reins. The mare had a bit of a limp in her right front leg and she was walking with her head low. It seemed as if the mare was in pain.

Lily jogged down the driveway. "What's wrong with Astra?"

Charlie shrugged. "I didn't do anything. Don't look at me like that."

"You rode her on the rocks, didn't you?" Lily sighed in exasperation.

Charlie looked away. "Everyone else rides on the rocks. What's your problem?"

"You know Astra needs to be in the soft dirt," she scolded in a low voice. She didn't want Mr. Henley to hear her over-stepping her bounds and acting like Astra's trainer.

"Here." Charlie handed her the reins. "If you know so much, you take her!"

Mr. Henley looked down from the back of his horse. "Charlie, mind your manners. Take your own horse back to the barn and give her a good brushing. I'm sure she'll be fine by tonight." He turned to Lily. "I'm afraid Charlie let her eat the old dead grass down by the marsh. I've told him a million times not to do that, but he doesn't listen."

"I couldn't stop her," Charlie protested. "She practically dragged me over to it and started pigging out. Now she's got a bellyache and it's her own fault." He tried handing the reins to Lily again.

"You'll cool this mare out yourself, son," Mr. Henley said in a stern voice. "Maybe next time you'll do what you're told. Let's go." He turned his horse toward the barn.

Meloney stepped off Jasper and walked beside Lily. "Char-

17

lie's so lazy," she said. "He didn't want the hassle of fighting with her."

"You mean, he just let her drop her head and eat?" Lily said, horrified.

"It sure looked like it." Meloney reined Jasper in a half circle. "Listen, I've got to head home, but I'm a little worried about Astra. That grass in the marsh is really bad. It's growing in stagnant water. I heard some other horses have gotten sick after eating there."

No, Lily thought, feeling a bit sick herself. *That can't happen to Astra.*

"They say it's a colic that comes on pretty quickly," Meloney went on. "I'll call you later to find out how she's doing."

Lily followed the Henleys back to the barn. In spite of Mr. Henley's warning that Charlie was responsible for cooling out Astra, Lily did all she could to help. While he brushed the mare, she got out the iodine and painted the bottoms of her hooves. Her mother used to do that to take out the sting and toughen them up. She offered Astra one of the mare's favorite molasses treats, but the horse only lipped it.

"I think she's got colic coming on," Lily told Mr. Henley when he came by to check on the mare. "Maybe we should keep her up in a stall for a few hours so we can check on her? I can call my grandma and tell her I'll be late for dinner."

"No need for that," Mr. Henley said. "I'm turning this bunch out in the pasture next to the house. I'll keep an eye on her. I'm sure she'll come out of this in an hour or two. She's got a little bit of indigestion, that's all. She'll be back in her stall tonight."

Lily had no choice but to stand back. As she watched her favorite horse walk off with her head drooped, she knew something was very wrong.

Three

ily went back to Whispering Pines Ranch after dinner that night. She found Mr. Henley inside Astra's stall giving her a dose of bute to make her more comfortable.

"Is she any better?" Lily asked.

Mr. Henley put the nozzle of the dosage syringe into Astra's mouth and pushed the plunger, then held her chin high so she wouldn't spit out the bitter, aspirin-like paste. "She's about the same. Maybe a little worse." He took off her halter and gave her a sympathetic pat. "I've got the vet coming out in the morning to take a look at her. Something is definitely wrong, but she's not sick enough for it to be anything serious. I think she just ate something that didn't agree with her."

The full hay net and the leftover grain in the feeder told Lily all she needed to know. She tried to convince herself it was just a mild bellyache, but Astra never left food in her feeder—especially grain.

"You go home and get some rest, Lily," Mr. Henley advised. "Dr. Tison will be here at nine tomorrow morning if you want to come by to watch him examine her. I know this horse means a lot to you. We'll take good care of her, and I'll tell Thomas to check on her during the night."

"Can I spend a few minutes with her before I go?" Lily asked.

Mr. Henley nodded. He walked out of the enclosure and held the door for Lily to enter. "Just make sure you lock up before you go. You know what an escape artist she is."

Lily walked quietly to the corner where Astra stood with her head down and her back leg cocked. The horse shifted uncomfortably from one leg to the other. "You okay, girl?" She took Astra's head in her hands, rubbing her large cheek-bones and staring into her soft brown eyes. "That medicine will help you. And if you still feel bad in the morning, Dr. Tison will be out to see you."

If anyone could help Astra get better, it was Dr. Tison, the kind young veterinarian. He'd come to their town after graduating from vet school and had built a thriving practice in only a few years. Then his National Guard unit got called overseas. He'd just recently returned home to his veterinarian job.

Dr. Tison had been the vet on duty when her mother and Astra had the accident. He'd been the one to help the medics with her mother as well as the mare. He knew Lily's story. He didn't think she was weird for being so attached to the gray Arabian mare. *You and your mom both believed in Astra's ability, and maybe you feel closer to your mother through this horse,* Dr. Tison had once told her. After giving it some thought, Lily had decided he was right.

Now she threw her arms around Astra's neck, holding on for several moments, seeking comfort in the horse's warmth and presence. Dr. Tison was totally right. When she spent time with Astra, she did feel a connection with her mom. It was the same way she'd felt the first time she sneaked into her mother's clothes closet after her dad went to work.

Every once in a while, she loved to worm her way between the hanging clothes and breathe in the wonderful scent of horses and wildflowers. It was probably just the lingering perfume of her mother's shampoo, but still, it was something left of *her*—and it smelled wonderful.

Lily always held onto that feeling, treasuring it and soaking out every last bit of warm, fuzzy emotion she could get. What if the day came when she couldn't feel her mother's presence anymore? That thought scared her senseless.

Astra shifted and Lily released her hold. "Get better, pretty. I'll be over to see you in the morning." Quietly, she let herself out of the stall and closed the door behind her.

Her father's truck was in the driveway by the time she got home. He hadn't made it back before dinner like he'd hoped. Even though it was his day off, he'd put in a full day of work. Before she went up to bed, Gram O'Neil had fixed him a plate of roast beef for supper and left it in the refrigerator for him to reheat when he got home. Lily took it out and popped it in the microwave, then sat down to tell her father about Astra.

"Lily, honey," Mr. O'Neil said, placing his large, work-calloused hand on top of her own. "I know that's your favorite horse, but she's no concern of mine. You know how I feel about horses, and *that* one in particular."

The bell on the microwave timer went off, saving Lily from an uncomfortable discussion—or a huge gap of silence. She put her father's dinner in front of him and said good night. She wanted to go to bed so she could get up early and make it to the ranch in time to talk to the vet. She kissed her dad and climbed the old wooden stairs to her room. After brushing her teeth and washing her face, she crawled into her warm bed and thought about the day's events.

It was strange how being around Astra made her feel closer to her mom, and yet the mare just reminded her dad of their loss. How could she make her father understand how much she loved this mare?

* * *

Lily woke to the sound of a vehicle coming up the road. She heard it hit the giant pothole in front of their house, bumping hard and grinding tires. She rolled over and looked at the alarm clock. Five thirty? The sun wouldn't be up for another hour at least. She wondered who would be traveling the back roads at this hour, and where the driver was headed. There were only a few more ranches on this road.

She tossed the covers back, noting that the house was much warmer than it had been yesterday morning. She peeked out the window and followed the receding taillights as they approached Whispering Pines Ranch. Her heart beat a little faster when she noticed several lights on in the barn. The Henleys usually didn't feed their horses until about eight o'clock. With a sinking feeling, Lily realized that the vehicle belonged to Dr. Tison.

Astra!

She scrambled into her clothing, almost tripping and falling when she couldn't get her foot into her pant leg. It could only mean one thing if the vet had been called at this hour of the morning…Astra had taken a turn for the worse.

She opened her bedroom door and tiptoed down the stairs, pausing in the living room to see if anyone was stirring. She thought about waking her dad to tell him where she was going. His room was just next door. But Lily knew he'd probably say she couldn't go. If he woke up to find her gone, he'd be worried and she'd probably be in big trouble when she got home. Maybe she should leave a note? She hesitated, unsure of what to do. All she knew was that Astra was in trouble and needed her.

"Lily?" Her grandmother's voice echoed from the stairwell. "Is everything okay? What are you doing up at this hour?"

"I'm okay, Grams." Lily could hear her grandmother's slippers pad down the stairs and swish toward her across the hardwood floor. In the darkness Lily could smell the familiar baby-powder scent that was purely Grandma O'Neil.

"The vet just pulled into the Henley place," Lily said. "He's not supposed to be there until nine. Something's wrong and I think it's Astra. I've got to get over there."

"Have you asked your father?" Grams pulled her robe tightly about her to ward off the night chill.

"No!" Lily held her breath, hoping the hastily blurted word didn't wake him. She could hear the question in her grandmother's sudden silence. "I'm afraid he'll say no if I ask. You know how he feels about Astra. But I think she's in real trouble, Grams. Why else would the vet be there at this hour?"

"But it's dark outside," her grandmother said. "You can't ride your bike over there now. What if there's a bear or a mountain lion out there?"

Lily paused. She hadn't thought about that. What were the chances? "It's been a long time since we've seen a bear or mountain lion down around the ranches, Gram. And the Henley place is only a couple of big pastures away."

Grams snorted in the dark and shuffled toward the kitchen. "You're so much like your mother, Lily-girl." She lifted the keys to her Pontiac off the peg. They jangled noisily in the quiet of the room. "Come on. I'll drop you off. I'll deal with your father when he wakes up."

Lily heaved a sigh of relief. She quickly gathered her gloves and jacket and helped her grandmother into her over-sized coat. The two of them crept out the back door and down the stairs into the starry night.

The barn lights burned brightly as they pulled up to the stable. "I'll probably stay here until it's light, Grams," Lily said. "I can walk home then. Thanks for giving me a ride."

"Well, okay," Grams said. "Good luck."

Lily stepped out of the car and waved good-bye.

As she walked toward the barn, she heard the murmur of voices from inside. From what she could tell, it sounded as if Mr. Henley, Dr. Tison, and Thomas were all there. Her heart sank when she slipped inside the barn and saw them gathered outside Astra's stall. As she approached, they looked up in surprise.

Dr. Tison, a big man with broad shoulders and a friendly face, towered over the other two men. She was sure he'd been a good soldier, but she was happy he'd come back to be their veterinarian again. Her mother had been very impressed with him and many of the ranchers in the area used his services.

But Lily didn't like the look on his face right now—like he had a secret he didn't want to tell because he knew how badly it might hurt her. She looked from him to Mr. Henley to Thomas, wishing someone would speak up and break the silence.

"Is she going to be okay?" Lily moved forward. Astra's heavy, labored breathing filled the air.

Dr. Tison stepped in front of Lily, blocking her path. He bent down to her eye level and placed a comforting hand on her shoulder. "Lily, I don't think you want to go in there.

Maybe it would be better if you remember her the way she was."

The way she *was*?

Lily's mind did a cartwheel. The vet had spoken about Astra like she was...dead. But that couldn't be true. She could hear the mare's ragged breaths coming from the stall. She gazed about frantically, searching for a clue that would tell her everything would be okay. This was just a bad dream. Her eyes widened at the sight of two large syringes full of pale pink liquid sitting atop the veterinarian's bag.

There was no doubt in Lily's mind what those were. Time moved in slow motion as she looked at each person's face, trying to determine the truth. It was there in all three sympathetic glances. Mr. Henley quickly looked away.

Her gaze cut back to the medical bag. She'd seen those shots before, when some unfortunate horse had broken a leg and had to be euthanized. The first large dose of sedative would be administered in the vein. In just a short amount of time it would slow and then stop the heart. The second shot would be given to make sure the procedure was final.

Astra—her mother's beautiful hope for a national champion—was about to be destroyed!

Four

ily began to panic. Her own ragged breaths rivaled Astra's. *This can't be happening,* she thought. She felt her knees go all wobbly.

Dr. Tison reached out to steady her. "Lily, are you okay?"

Mr. Henley stepped forward and took her arm. "Lily, I'm going to take you home. You shouldn't be here for this, especially at this hour of the morning. What in the world were you thinking, honey?" He pulled his keys from his pocket and motioned for her to follow him out of the barn.

Lily just stood there, shaking. She couldn't leave.

She *wouldn't* leave.

If she did, they'd put Astra to sleep for sure. Maybe she was only a kid, but she planned to do everything in her power to keep them from putting down the mare. "I don't want to go home," she said. "Astra needs me."

"You should go with Mr. Henley." Dr. Tison gave her a sympathetic look, then pointed her in the direction of the barn door. "Leave this to me. I'll make sure she doesn't feel any pain, I promise. Let Steven take you home to your dad and grandma."

Lily tried not to feel betrayed. Dr. Tison knew how much Astra meant to her. She looked to Thomas for some kind of help. He gave her a sorrowful nod and went back to the tack room.

Mr. Henley called from the doorway, "Lily, come on! Let's get you home."

"I'm not leaving." Lily crossed her arms, determined to make a stand.

"Give us a minute, would you, Steve?" Dr. Tison said, his brows knit in concern.

Lily choked back the tears clogging her throat. She tried desperately to hold them at bay, but she could feel them spilling down her cheeks. Dr. Tison pulled a handkerchief out of his pocket and handed it to her.

"What happened to her?" Lily accepted the handkerchief, but instead of using it to wipe her tears or blow her nose, she wadded and twisted it with her hands. "Astra was fine when she left for her workout yesterday. She was just a little gimpy from Charlie riding her in the rocks more than he should have. And she ate that bad grass. How did she go from that t-to this?" Lily hiccuped.

Dr. Tison sighed and squatted down on his heels in front of Astra's stall. "Truth is, I don't know." He ran a hand over his short, military-style haircut. "I suspect she ate something poisonous. I've drawn blood for a chemistry panel so we can figure out what's wrong. But that will take several hours to come back, and she's so far gone Mr. Henley decided to have her put down now."

Lily's heart faltered in her chest. "You can't!" she cried. "There's got to be something you can do. You went to veterinary college. You're smart..." A tremble started deep inside her and worked its way outward, causing her whole body to shake.

The vet took off his coat and placed it around her shoulders, then stood and peered over the stall door at Astra. He rubbed his hand across his brow as if he were trying to scrub away a tough decision. "I've done everything I can think of, Lily. I've filled her with the best medicines, but nothing is working. There's been no change at all, except a worsening of all her vital signs." He turned back to Lily. "I know how much this horse means to you, but it's time to let her go."

Lily froze, afraid to breathe or even blink. Maybe if she stood motionless, the world would stop, too? Astra would be fine, and everything would go back to normal.

Mr. Henley called from the doorway, his voice roughened with impatience. "Lily, let's leave Dr. Tison to do his job. It's time to go."

Memories raced across Lily's mind: seeing her mother on Astra, their talks about placing Astra in the Tevis Cup, her own hopes to take over that dream someday and make her mom proud…

She turned to look back at Mr. Henley. He watched her expectantly, his car keys jingling as he tapped them against his leg.

With sudden clarity, Lily knew what she had to do. She bolted for the stall door, dodging around the surprised vet, and swung the door open just enough for her to squeeze through it.

"Lily, come back here!" Dr. Tison's voice echoed through the quiet barn. Several horses nickered in alarm.

The reality of seeing Astra lying in the middle of her stall stopped Lily in her tracks. The mare's sides rose and fell with each struggling breath. Sweat marks darkened her neck and flanks, and the shavings around her were strewn wildly about as if she had been running in her dreams—or nightmares.

Lily dropped to her knees and threw her arms around the mare's neck, pressing her cheek into Astra's mane. She gave up trying to hold back the tears and let them flow freely. "You can't die, girl. It's not fair! You've still got the Tevis Cup to run in. You're going to make us all proud."

Mr. Henley and the vet entered the stall. Lily thought they might try to forcibly remove her. She hung on tight to Astra, choking on the tears that ran down the back of her throat.

"For heaven's sake, Lily. What in the world are you doing?" Mr. Henley placed his hands on his hips and sighed in exasperation. "You're only postponing the inevitable with these stalling tactics."

"Steven…" Dr. Tison shot him a glance that said he didn't approve of the owner's approach.

"She *can* get better," Lily hiccuped again. "You've got to give her a chance! I know Dr. Tison can save her." She looked up at the vet, but her eyes were blurred with tears and she couldn't read his expression. "P-please?" It was all she could utter before huge, choking sobs took over, threatening to cut off her air.

Mr. Henley reached down to help Lily up, but the big veterinarian stayed his hand. "Let her be, Steven. Can't you see the poor kid is miserable? This was her mother's favorite horse and we're about to put her down."

"I realize that," Mr. Henley said. "But the best thing to do for her is to take her home so she can be with her family. And it's not fair to the horse to make her suffer longer. The quicker we can put her down, the better off everyone will be."

"Astra isn't in any pain," the vet said. "She's more or less in a comatose state. Letting her remain a few more hours isn't going to hurt anything. And it might help Lily here."

Lily tried to give the vet a thankful smile but she couldn't force her mouth to turn upward. She sniffed loudly instead.

"I don't know, Dale…," Mr. Henley said slowly.

"Please, Mr. Henley?" Lily managed to whisper.

The ranch owner placed a hand on her shoulder. "I know how much Astra means to you," he began. "And you might think I'm being heartless. But I'm trying to do what's best for all concerned."

Lily sat up and took several steadying breaths, trying to bring herself to speak. Her chest hurt so badly she thought her heart would explode. She ran her coat sleeve across her eyes and cleared her throat. "This is the horse my mother was going to prove in the Tevis. *It was her dream.* And now you want to put her to sleep, and none of that dream will ever be able to come true!"

Mr. Henley shook his head. "I'm really, truly sorry, Lily… about your mom, and about Astra, too. Your mom was a very special person, and a great rider. I have no doubt that the pair of them would have done well in the Tevis Cup." He paused for a moment. "Maybe there's something I can do for you. It isn't much, but it might help lessen the hurt."

He turned and walked out of the stall, returning a few minutes later with a piece of paper in his hands. He pulled a pen out of his pocket and signed the paper, then handed it to Lily.

"What's this?" Lily took the paper he offered. Her eyes grew wide when she recognized the Arabian Horse Association registration papers. She sniffed. "I don't understand…"

"I believe that Steve here wants to give you a gift," Dr. Tison said, with a small, sad smile.

Mr. Henley nodded. "Those are Astra's registration papers. I've signed them over to you. She's yours for the next couple of hours. But if the mare doesn't show improvement soon, I'll have to insist that Dale go ahead and put her down. I know it might seem harsh, but it's what's best for the animal." Without another word, he turned and walked out of the barn.

Lily was too dumbstruck to respond.

Dr. Tison waited a few moments for Lily to regain some composure, then leaned against the door as he spoke. "So how does it feel to be a horse owner again?"

Lily studied the papers through swollen eyes. She ran her fingers over the place where Mr. Henley had written her name. Astra Atomica was hers now. Really and truly hers—at least for the next several hours. She ran her hand lovingly down the prone mare's coat. "Did you hear that, girl? You're my horse."

Astra gave no response but Lily was sure the mare could hear her. She talked to her in a soothing voice. "You're going to get better, girl. Don't you worry. All of that medicine is going to kick in and you're going to start getting better."

She thought about what would happen if by some miracle Astra did recover. Her dad would have a fit. Mr. Henley probably would, too. The thought almost made her smile. She knew giving her Astra had been just a symbolic gesture meant to make her feel better. And it was a nice thing for the owner to do. But in Mr. Henley's mind, Astra was already dead.

Dr. Tison opened the stall door. "I'll give her another shot and check her heart rate and temperature," he offered. "Then I'm going to make a few other house calls in the area. Might as well start the day early. I'll be back in a couple of hours and we'll see what Mr. Henley wants to do then."

Lily nodded. She sat back while the veterinarian checked Astra and gave her another shot.

"Her heart rate is still elevated, and her temperature is 103°," Dr. Tison said. "At this point, there's not much we can do for her except make her comfortable."

Lily looked at the sick mare. Sweat marks and dirt stains

marred her shiny coat from when she'd tossed and turned. "Can I get a brush and some warm water and clean her up a bit?"

Dr. Tison shrugged. "I guess it can't hurt. Keep your chin up, kiddo, and I'll see you in a few hours." He patted her on the shoulder and let himself out of the stall.

Lily went to the wash rack and drew a small amount of warm water, then picked up the brush bucket. If Astra was going to die, she wanted her to at least be clean and comfortable. The thought brought back tears and she swallowed hard.

As she wandered back to the stall, Lily could hear the sounds of a waking barn. Horses pawed at stall doors, begging for morning feed. Grain buckets rattled as grooms unstacked them and lined them up for filling. She could hear the hushed voices of Jill and Thomas down the way and knew that the barn manager had filled Jill in on the details about Astra.

Lily let herself into the enclosure and went to work brushing the mare down. The weather was still cold, so she didn't want to put too much water on her—just enough to get her clean. Several times, Astra twitched or released a small groan, causing Lily to wonder if she might wake up. It felt odd to watch the horse lying there, barely breathing, when only the day before she'd been tossing her proud head, eager to be off for a run.

Jill popped her head over the door. "How's she doing?" She took a look at the mare and shook her head. "Oh, Lily. I'm so sorry."

Lily gave her a grateful smile. "No, I'm sorry. It's your horse."

"Not anymore," Jill said. "Astra was very special to you. I'm glad my dad turned her papers over to you."

When Jill left, Charlie appeared. Lily cringed inwardly, sure that he'd say something to wreck the moment.

"Hey, Lily." He tipped his chin in her direction, his eyes cast down. "I'll do your stalls for you today."

He turned and walked away, shoulders slumped. Lily wondered if he felt responsible for what had happened to Astra. Part of her wanted to blame him for all of this. But she remembered how many times she'd let her old pony tug her to different places to crop grass. She couldn't put the entire blame on Charlie. Horses got sick. And sometimes they died. That was the way of things. But not Astra. Not now.

Lily finished brushing Astra and spent the rest of the time petting her and speaking softly. She quietly talked about the memories she had of her mother and the beautiful gray mare. She was dimly aware of the barn activities around her, but everyone left her alone.

Occasionally Astra would take a deeper breath, or twitch a muscle, and Lily felt a flicker of hope. Maybe the horse would come out of this. She'd heard of people who'd come out of a coma after years of sleep. Miracles were always possible, weren't they?

But all too quickly, the time passed. Soon she felt the presence of Mr. Henley and Dr. Tison in front of Astra's stall.

"It's time, Lily," Mr. Henley said.

Lily stood and placed herself between them and Astra. Again, she knew what she had to do. Astra needed time—just a little more time to see if she could get better. They were all reacting too quickly. Dr. Tison had said the mare wasn't in pain. Why the hurry to put her down? Why not give her a chance?

"No," she said quietly but firmly.

Mr. Henley looked confused. "What do you mean, *no*?" He

motioned for her to leave the stall. "Come on out of there, Lily, and let's get this over with."

Lily planted her feet. "No. Astra is my horse now. You gave her to me." She turned to Dr. Tison. "You can't put her down without the owner's permission, right?" She thought she saw a glimmer of admiration in the vet's eyes. It gave her courage to stand her ground.

Dr. Tison nodded in agreement.

"I'm sorry, Mr. Henley. I know you think this is what's best for the horse. But it's not. We've got to give Astra a little more time." She turned back to Dr. Tison. "She's my horse now," she repeated. "You saw the registration papers with my name on them. I want to give her a chance. I don't want her put to sleep."

Mr. Henley opened his mouth to speak, but the veterinarian put his hand on the ranch owner's shoulder and guided him away from the stall.

Lily stood as still as she could, listening to their receding footsteps and hushed words, not daring to move a single muscle. She hadn't realized she'd been holding her breath until it all came out in a big whoosh. She collapsed to her knees in the center of the stall and sucked in big gulps of air. She wasn't sure where she'd gotten the courage to stand up to Mr. Henley and fight for Astra's life. But she'd done it.

Lily crawled to where Astra lay, quiet and still in the deep bed of shavings. She reached out a shaky hand and stroked the warm, gray coat. She wasn't sure if she'd done the right thing. Only time would tell. But at least now they might have a little more of it.

She'd done her part. Now the rest was up to Astra.

Five

The stall door opened and Lily quickly waved her friend inside. Meloney tucked her wavy blonde hair behind her ears and knelt in the shavings next to Lily. Her cheeks glowed pink, as if she'd run all the way there.

"How is she?" Meloney leaned forward and ran her hand along Astra's neck. "I can't believe she went downhill so fast. Charlie feels really bad about the whole thing."

Lily sat with Astra's head in her lap, frowning at the mention of Charlie's name. She couldn't help blaming him.

Meloney shifted to a more comfortable position. "I'm not sticking up for the guy, but it could have happened to any of us. I let Jasper stop to eat and drink not far from where Charlie and Astra were. It could be Jasper lying here now instead of Astra."

"It doesn't matter," Lily said. "Astra's going to get better. She deserves a little more time to see if we can figure out a way to save her. Maybe there's a medicine Dr. Tison hasn't tried yet."

"Is it true that Mr. Henley gave you Astra, and you stopped them from putting her down?" Meloney asked, a note of awe in her voice.

Smiling, Lily pulled Astra's papers from her coat pocket and showed them to her friend. "My mom would be really happy. She wouldn't have let them put Astra down either. Mr. Henley thinks I'm doing the wrong thing, but I know Astra can make it. She's fighting for her life."

"So what are you going to do?" Meloney asked. "What's your dad going to say when he finds out?"

Lily bit her lip. She hadn't thought about her father's reaction in a while—she'd been too concerned about Astra. He wouldn't be happy when he found out that the mare was now hers.

A knock sounded on the stall door and Dr. Tison peered in. "How's the patient doing?"

"She moved a little bit," Lily said hopefully.

Meloney stood and dusted off her pants, but Lily stayed where she was. The vet let himself into the stall, his brow creased in concern. He turned to Meloney.

"Do you mind if I have a few minutes with Lily?" he asked.

Meloney gave Lily an encouraging smile and left the stall.

Dr. Tison knelt down next to Lily. She swallowed hard at the grim look on his face.

"Lily, I want you to know that I'm doing my best," Dr. Tison said. "But sometimes, our best isn't good enough. There's not much left I can do. I thought we'd try another IV drip on her. She could use the fluids and another dose of medicine, but I think we're chasing rainbows."

Lily turned away, ordering herself not to cry. She felt the warmth of Astra's head in her lap and saw the shallow rise and fall of the mare's rib cage. Astra was still here and she wasn't in pain. That meant there was hope, didn't it?

"She was a good mare," the vet said. "And she meant a lot to you and your mother, so it's worth a try. But if we don't see an improvement in a couple more hours, you need to think seriously about letting her go. At that point, it would be cruel to keep her going." He leaned over and gave her an encouraging hug. "I know your mother wouldn't want that, and neither do you."

Dr. Tison stood and reached for the medical supplies he'd brought into the stall with him. Lily gently lifted Astra's head, and moved to the corner so the vet could work unhindered.

Lily watched him run the IV and thought about all the medical care Astra would need if she pulled through this. What had she gotten herself into? Where would she get the money to pay the vet? Her father certainly didn't have it. Neither did her grandmother. And her dad definitely wouldn't pay for anything having to do with Astra.

"Dr. Tison, I don't know how I'm going to pay for this," she said in a small voice. "I've only saved up eighty dollars from my allowance, but you can have it." She scuffed at the stall floor with the toe of her boot. "I'll get a job doing something. I'll find a way to pay you. I promise. You've got to help her."

Dr. Tison put a stethoscope to Astra's rib cage, listening to her heart. "Let's work at making her well first. Then we'll worry about who's paying and how much, okay?" He hung the IV bag on a nail in the wall. "It's going to take about an hour for all of this to run through. Why don't you go home and rest up?"

Lily thought about the ugly scene that was sure to take place when she told her dad she now owned Astra. It would be easier to stay here at the barn and not deal with her father, but she knew she'd have to do it sooner or later. Better he heard it from her. She nodded to the vet and let herself out of the stall. "Please take good care of her."

"I'll do my best, Lily, but I can't promise you she won't pass while you're gone," Dr. Tison said. "I can only promise you that I won't euthanize her. She's hung on this long. I don't think another hour will make a difference."

Meloney, who was still waiting outside, followed Lily down the barn aisle. "Jasper is ready to go home. We can walk you home if you want."

Lily nodded. "Okay, but there's something I've got to do first." She went in search of Mr. Henley and found him in Contina's stall. "Mr. Henley, sir?" She shoved her hands into her jeans pockets. "I know you don't approve of what I'm doing, but this is something I have to do…for my mom and Astra and me."

Mr. Henley looked at her over the top of Contina's back and nodded. "I don't agree with your outlook on Astra's chances for survival, Lily, but I do understand."

The ranch owner went back to brushing Contina. "And I know it took a lot of courage to come and tell me that," he said. "Thank you."

Lily took that as her cue to leave. She nodded and hurried out of the barn to find Meloney and Jasper. Her friend pulled on the bay gelding's reins and they walked together toward Lily's house.

"What are you going to tell your dad?" Meloney asked.

Lily sighed. "I guess there's nothing I can do but tell him the truth."

"He won't let you keep her," Meloney predicted. "Especially since it's Astra." She shook her head. "You're in major trouble."

"Thanks a lot, Ms. Obvious," Lily said. She saw Meloney's shoulders slump and instantly felt bad for snipping at her friend. Meloney had her best interests at heart. "I'm sorry, Mel. I'm just tired and worried."

Meloney gave her a smile over her shoulder. "No, I'm sorry. I know how rotten you must be feeling. I need to learn to keep my mouth shut sometimes." She turned Jasper down Lily's driveway and stopped at the front door. "Do you want me to come in with you?" she offered. "Maybe your dad won't yell much if you have company."

"Thanks," Lily said. "But I think I better handle this one alone. Besides," she added with a grin, "I don't want any witnesses when I get chewed out times ten."

"Well, I sure hope you don't get grounded for life," Meloney said, picking up the reins.

Lily made a shooing motion with her hands. "If I do, you'll have to take care of Astra for me and ride her in the Tevis Cup." She ran up the porch stairs and paused on the top step. "I'll call you if I can and let you know what happens," she said.

"Good luck, Lil. I'll keep my cell phone on." Meloney turned Jasper and they trotted down the driveway.

Mustering her courage, Lily pushed open the door and stepped inside. The house smelled like bacon and eggs.

"Is that you, Lily?" her grandmother's voice called.

"Yeah, Grams, it's me." She took her boots off in the hallway and hung her coat on the hook. She glanced at the clock. Nine fifteen. So much had happened since sunrise.

"Your father and I are eating breakfast. Come in and have a bite with us and tell us what the big to-do is at the Henley place," Grams said.

From the hallway, Lily could hear her grandmother taking out another plate. She was probably loading it with crisp bacon and fluffy eggs, not knowing that Lily wouldn't be able to stomach a bite of it. Lily stood there for a few moments longer, not sure what she would tell her dad. What could she say that wouldn't throw him into a fit? *Hi, Dad. I know you don't like horses and really don't want me anywhere near them, but we're now the proud owners of an Arabian endurance mare. So get used to the idea, okay?*

"Hurry up, Flower, your breakfast is getting cold," her father called to her.

Lily walked into the kitchen and took her place at the table. Just as she suspected, her grandma had loaded her plate with scrambled eggs. She pushed them around with her fork for a while, listening to her dad make small talk. She took a big bite of bacon, hoping they wouldn't see how nervous she was.

"So, Lily," Grams said. "What was the big excitement at the Henley place this morning? Anything to do with your favorite horse?"

The bacon suddenly lodged in Lily's throat, refusing to go down. She grabbed her glass of milk and took several big swallows. "Astra's sick and she's in big trouble," Lily blurted out, as soon as she could speak. "Dr. Tison's not even sure what happened, but she may...die." Lily nearly choked again.

Her dad paused mid-chew. "I'm really sorry to hear that, Lily. I know how much you care about that horse."

Lily's head jerked up in surprise at her father's compassionate tone. Now was the time to deliver the news, she decided. If she were lucky, she wouldn't be grounded for the rest of her life. Maybe just half of it.

Six

ily winced as her father's fork clattered to the table. "What do you mean, he *gave* you Astra?" Her father's eyes bulged with disbelief. "You can't just *give* somebody a horse. Especially *that* one! It's not like giving away a puppy or a kitten."

"Now, Daniel," Grams said. "Calm down for a minute, please. I'm sure we can figure this out."

Lily stared at the table. She should have just kept quiet and figured out another way to tell her dad.

"What part of *no more horses* didn't you understand, Lily?" Her father ran a hand over his face. "We discussed this. You know the rules."

Lily folded her hands in her lap, willing the tears to stay behind her eyes. "I didn't ask for her." Lily thought her voice sounded small and unsure, but she pressed on. "Mr. Henley gave her to me because he thinks she's dying, and he thought it would make me happy to own her for a little while." Lily looked her father in the eye while she reached into her pocket for Astra's papers and laid them on the table. "Mom would have been happy for me."

She pushed her chair back from the table and ran to her room, barely making it to the bed before sobs tore from her throat. Burying her head under her pillow, she let the tears soak the sheets. It was so unfair! All of it…her mother, her dad's unreasonable demands, losing Astra.

Lily felt a weight lower onto the bed beside her. It was so like her grandma to come comfort her when she felt sad. But the weight next to her was too heavy to be her grandmother. She was startled when she realized it was her father.

"I'm sorry, Lily." He patted her shoulder. "My first reaction to that news wasn't very good. I just spoke to Mr. Henley on the phone and he told me all about it. I'm still not happy about this, but this isn't a good time to argue about it. I think you'd better get back over there."

Lily sat up and rubbed her sleeve across her eyes, sniffing back the excess tears. "Is Astra okay?"

Her father shrugged. "In her case, I'm not really sure what you'd call okay. But Dr. Tison said she's still hanging in there." He stood and stretched. "Come on, I'll get my keys and take you back to the barn."

Surprised by her dad's understanding, Lily swung her feet over the side of the bed and stood on wobbly legs. "Everyone thinks she's going to die," she said. Now that she'd uttered the words out loud, her legs felt even more unsteady.

Her father put an arm around her shoulder and directed her to the doorway. "Let's just wait and see what happens. If Astra makes it through this, we'll sit down and discuss how we're going to deal with it."

Lily felt herself brighten. Discussing it was a start.

"Don't get your hopes up too much, kiddo," her father warned. "I haven't changed my mind on this matter. I don't want you riding. If Astra makes it, we'll have to talk to Mr.

Henley and see if he'll take her back. Even if I were okay with having another horse, you know we couldn't afford it right now. Things have been really tough since your mom died."

Lily felt her new hopes plummet to the ground, collecting around her feet like dead leaves from a winter tree. She needed to forget about the what-ifs. For now she needed to concentrate on Astra making it through the day.

* * *

Lily stepped from the warm truck, her breath frosting the air. She waved good-bye to her father and headed toward the barn. Dr. Tison's pickup was still parked out front. Anxious to hear what he had to say, she hurried to the door.

Lily's dad rolled down his window. "Lily? Can you come back here for a moment?"

She stopped and walked back to the truck.

"Despite how I feel about this horse, and this whole situation, I do understand how important Astra is to you." He paused and looked at her for several moments. "Are you going to be okay if the mare doesn't make it?"

Her father's words warmed her heart, but Lily frowned anyway. Would she be okay? Losing Astra wouldn't be anything like it had been when she lost her mother. A horse wasn't the same as a parent. But it would be a lot more pain than she wanted to deal with. "We won't have to worry about that," Lily told her father firmly. "She's going to make it." She turned back to the barn, waving over her shoulder as her dad put the truck in reverse and backed away.

Once inside the barn, she went straight to Astra's stall. The vet stood outside the door. "How's she doing?" Lily asked, poking her head over the door. She scanned the mare for signs of stress in her breathing.

Dr. Tison let himself out of the stall and leaned on the door with Lily. "Well, with your extra-special care, she's still hanging in there. I'm going to keep trying."

Lily stood quietly for several moments and then turned to the vet. "They say people in a coma can still hear you. Do you think Astra can hear me when I talk to her?"

"I think she probably can," the vet said, sounding tired. It was only three o'clock, but he'd been here since five in the morning. "Maybe you should go brush her up and talk to her again. I'll check on some of the other horses. Might as well while I'm here."

Grabbing the brush bucket, Lily let herself into the stall. "Hey, girl." She knelt in the bedding beside the mare and ran her hand lovingly down the long, gray neck. It might have been her imagination, but Lily could have sworn that Astra seemed to relax and breathe easier.

She picked up a soft brush, running it over the mare's coat, flicking away the dirt and bedding. What would she do tomorrow when she was expected to be in school? No way would her dad let her skip classes to be with Astra. She placed her hand on the mare's neck. It seemed cooler to her touch. A flicker of hope zipped through Lily's insides. "Dr. Tison?" she called down the shed row.

The vet was by her side in a moment. "What is it, Lily?"

She ran her hands over the rest of Astra's body. Yes, she definitely felt cooler. Did that mean she was getting better? "I think her fever is breaking."

Dr. Tison took the thermometer from his pocket and took Astra's temperature. He held it to the light to read it. "Yep. Looks like she's come down almost two degrees."

"What does that mean?" Lily asked anxiously.

Dr. Tison grabbed his stethoscope and listened to Astra's breathing. "Well, without new blood work I can't be sure," he said. "She might be getting better—or it's possible that some of her organs are starting to shut down."

Lily felt like someone had just punched her in the stomach. "Shutting down?"

"We can do more blood work, but I don't think it'll do any good," Dr. Tison answered. "Mr. Henley won't put any more money into her, and I don't think your dad would be willing to pay for it, either. Besides, it would take a while for the results to come back. We'll just have to wait and see. In a few more hours, she'll either be better, or she'll be gone."

Lily knew the vet was right. There was no sense in doing more tests.

"I've done everything I can, Lily." Dr. Tison began putting his equipment back in the medical bag. "The rest is up to Astra. I'm going to go see some other patients. I'll be back to check on Astra in two hours."

The veterinarian closed his bag and looked Lily straight in the eye. She felt the weight of his words all the way down to her toes.

"When I return, if Astra isn't better, you need to be prepared to do the right thing." He turned and walked down the shed row toward the exit.

The right thing? Lily raised her brows and pondered the vet's words for a moment. Wasn't she doing the right thing now by keeping Astra alive? But deep in her heart she knew what Dr. Tison meant. She tried to prepare herself mentally for the two-hour wait.

She situated herself again so Astra's head lay in her lap. She spoke soft, encouraging words to the horse while running her hands over the mare's perfectly dished face and neck. "Spring is coming, and I know how you love to run through the fields and graze on all that new grass. Just hang in there and get stronger and you'll get your chance to do it again. I *know* you're getting better, girl. Just, please…" Lily's voice cracked. "*Please* give me some sort of sign that you're improving so we've got something to show Dr. Tison when he comes back."

The door rattled and Lily looked up to see Charlie entering the stall. Her cheeks turned pink when she realized that he'd probably heard her private words to Astra. She lifted her chin and waited for some smart-aleck comment. Instead, he grabbed the feed bucket from the corner and turned it upside down to sit on, looking very sad.

Charlie stayed there for several moments, not saying a word. He just stared at the prone mare, unwilling to meet Lily's eyes. Lily shifted uncomfortably. She wasn't sure what to say to him, either, so she let the silence stretch out between them.

"I'm really sorry, Lily." Charlie's voice was so quiet, she could barely hear it. "Astra is going to die, and it's all my fault. I know she's your favorite." He grabbed a stem of hay out of the feeder and picked at it, still refusing to look at Lily.

Lily wasn't quite sure how to react. Part of her *did* want to blame him for all of Astra's woes, but she knew better. "I already told you, it's not your fault," Lily said.

"Yes, it is." Charlie rose to his feet. "My dad told me not to let her eat over by the marsh. But when Astra started tugging me that way, I was lazy and just let her go."

Now Lily was even more surprised. This was a new side of Charlie. She couldn't believe he'd volunteered himself as the scapegoat. She wanted so badly to blame him for Astra's misfortune. She didn't like the boy very much. It would be so easy to heap all the blame on him. Astra was lying there, maybe only an hour away from death, all because he'd been too lazy to steer her away from a bunch of bad grass.

She gently moved the mare's head from her lap and stood, brushing the bedding from her jeans. "Maybe there were some things you could have done differently, Charlie, but who knows? It might not have made a difference. Astra could've just as easily eaten something in her hay that caused the trouble. We'll probably never know."

She didn't know why she was being so nice to him.

Charlie attempted a smile. "You mean you don't hate me?"

Lily had to think pretty hard on that one. But she remembered her mother saying that she should never hate anyone. Hate was such a strong word. No, she didn't *hate* Charlie, but she sure didn't like him a whole lot, either. His apology helped some, though. If Astra made it through this, she'd be willing to forgive him anything. "No, Charlie, I don't hate you."

"Thanks, Lily."

Charlie shoved his hands into his pockets and gave her that cute grin that made him popular with the girls at school. Lily had never been dumb enough to fall for it.

"I always thought you were kind of a, you know…" Charlie hesitated, looking for the right word. "Well, a loner and kind of a dork," he said. "But you're really not so bad."

Lily fought the urge to pick up a road apple and bounce it off Charlie's head. "You should have just stopped at *thanks*," she told him. She shook her head, moving toward the stall door. But a loud groan, followed by a rustling of bedding, stopped Lily in her tracks.

"Whoa," Charlie said, his eyes widening.

Lily turned in time to see Astra's eyes open for a brief second, then close again as the gray mare took a deep breath and exhaled with a loud puff.

Lily felt a surge of hope. She wasn't sure what this change of circumstances meant. But one thing was for certain: between the fever subsiding and Astra opening her eyes, she could definitely argue for giving the mare more time.

Seven

Charlie, call Dr. Tison!" Lily ordered as she stumbled to Astra's side and dropped to her knees. She ran her hand over the mare's large cheekbone and Astra's eyes flickered open again for a brief moment. "Good girl." She spoke softly, encouraging the horse to come back to her.

Astra took a deep breath and let out another long groan. "Easy, girl," Lily crooned, her heart breaking at the thought of the mare being in pain now that she was awake. Lily looked up to see Charlie still standing there, gawking. "What are you doing? Get going!" Lily practically yelled. "We need Dr. Tison here now!"

Charlie ran from the stall and pounded down the barn aisle. Lily could hear him talking excitedly to someone in the tack room, most likely his sister or Thomas. A few moments later, Jill let herself into the stall and settled in the bedding beside Lily. "Is it true? Did Astra really open her eyes?"

Lily nodded. "Twice, and now she seems to be breathing a little heavier. I think the medication is wearing off. She seems to be having some pain."

Jill reached out and smoothed Astra's tangled mane into place. "I called Dr. Tison. He's on his way."

"Thanks, Jill."

They sat in silence, waiting for the vet to arrive. Charlie hovered outside the stall, kicking at stray pieces of hay and tossing pebbles down the barn aisle.

Word traveled quickly and soon Mr. Henley poked his head into the stall. "Dr. Tison just pulled in. So Astra's waking up?" He eyed the still form of the mare dubiously and looked Lily straight in the face. "This isn't another stalling tactic, is it?"

For a brief moment, Lily felt insulted. But she knew that if they did insist on putting Astra to sleep, she'd come up with every excuse in the book to give the mare more time. She couldn't blame Mr. Henley for asking.

She opened her mouth to answer, but Jill intervened. "Charlie saw her open her eyes. She's fighting hard to live, Dad."

Lily heard footsteps coming down the barn aisle, and Mr. Henley opened the stall door for Dr. Tison.

"So, she's coming around, is she?" The vet knelt beside the mare and pulled his stethoscope from around his neck, listening to Astra's heartbeat. Then he moved his stethoscope to several other spots, checking out Astra's heart and lung functions.

"She opened her eyes," Charlie said. "And she groaned really loud."

As if on cue, Astra grunted and twitched an ear. Everyone gasped in surprise.

Dr. Tison finished his examination and stood, pulling the stethoscope from his ears. He looked at Lily and smiled. "Her heartbeat is stronger and steady. Her breathing rate is elevated, but at this point, that's a good thing." He winked at Lily. "I guess we can probably do that blood test now. It looks like Astra might live long enough for us to read it."

The mare's eyes fluttered open again and she looked about the room. This time she didn't close them immediately. A murmur of appreciation went up from those gathered around the stall. Astra was improving!

"I'll go get the things I need to draw the blood sample."

Lily listened to Dr. Tison's footsteps recede into the distance. When he returned, someone else was with him. Lily was surprised to see her father's concerned face peering over the door.

"How are things going?" Mr. O'Neil asked.

"Well, Dan, this brave little mare seems to be doing better." He quickly drew the blood sample and slipped the vial into the protective carrier. "She's not out of danger yet, and I'll know more once I run this sample. But at the moment, I'd say she's got a decent chance of pulling through."

Mr. Henley looked doubtful. "The question is, will she ever be good for anything? Her liver is probably so damaged that she'll never be strong enough for work. And she might need continual medical care. If it were my horse, I'd still have her put down. It's really the most humane thing for her."

"She *is* your horse, Steven," Lily's father said quietly. "I didn't want to say anything earlier because my daughter was so upset. It was a generous offer, and we thank you, but we can't accept this horse. We don't have the money to care for her, and we don't have any stalls set up at home. You're going to have to take her back. Lily can bring you the registration papers later."

Lily jumped to her feet, which was a big mistake. Her legs wobbled so badly, she nearly toppled over. She felt like she'd just gone over a tall jump and her horse had dropped out from under her.

"*No!*" she cried, when she finally found her voice. She

turned to her father. "We can't give her back to Mr. Henley. He just said he'd probably put her down." She grabbed her father's arm. "Dad, Astra has fought so hard to stay alive. She's waking up now. We can't let her be put to sleep."

Mr. O'Neil breathed a heavy sigh. "Lily, we have nowhere to keep this horse, and no way to pay for her care."

It was almost as if she were on stage, with all eyes directed at her. Lily didn't want to cry in front of all these people, but a tear trickled down her cheek. She knew it would be followed by many more. She hated being a crybaby. "But, Dad," she whimpered. "This was Mom's favorite horse. She's *my* favorite horse. We can't just let her die—not after she's fought so hard to live."

"You can keep her here until you get a stall fixed at your house," Charlie volunteered.

Lily's father shook his head. "That still wouldn't solve the money issue. Times are tough in our household. I don't have the money to spend on a horse...especially a sick one."

"I can work," Lily said, amazed that her voice still worked. Tears gathered in her throat, making it difficult to speak. "I'll get a job mowing lawns or babysitting or something. I can pay for Astra's feed."

Jill hooked arms with her father, anchoring him to the spot as if she were afraid he might flee. "We could pay Lily to work for us. We're losing a groom next week. Lily could take his place." She poked her dad in the ribs for good measure.

Mr. Henley thought for a minute. "Lily is a good worker," he said, nodding. "She could come for a few hours after school, and work the weekends." He handed Lily a tissue. "Young lady, I think you're going to put a lot of time and money into a horse that won't even be rideable, but I understand her sentimental value to you. The job is yours if you want it, Lily."

"But there are already so many vet bills," Mr. O'Neil said, frowning. "From the sound of it, there are likely to be many more. And Lily could still lose the mare anyway."

Dr. Tison shrugged. "I'm not going to lie to you. If she pulls through, it's going to be very tough going with this horse. And Steven is right. Chances are, Astra might never be strong enough to carry a rider—even one as small as Lily."

Lily wanted to scream and throw things around the barn. What was the matter with the adults here? Everyone wanted to talk about the worst possible scenario. What about the *best* outcome? What if Astra got well and she *could* ride her? Well, if her father ever lifted his no-riding rule, anyway.

"I don't care!" Lily shouted to be heard over all the discussion. "This was my mother's favorite horse. She was going to make her a national champion. Even if Astra can't do anything more than walk and crop grass, I want her! That's what my mom would want. Don't you understand?"

She stared at each of them in turn. Surely, at least one person here could understand what she was going through? Didn't they see how important this was?

"Lily…" Her father spread his hands in a hopeless gesture.

"If money is the problem, I'll donate the veterinary work," Dr. Tison volunteered. "Your family trusted me, Dan, when I first got out of vet school. You've been friends and clients of mine for many years. I know how important this is to Lily—and would have been to her mother. It's the least I could do in memory of her."

"Please, Dad," Lily begged. If her father didn't say yes, she didn't know what she'd do. "I'll work really hard. You won't have to spend any money on Astra. I'm all she has now. I can't let her die."

Her father didn't answer. She could see the war going on inside him. He knew how much this horse meant to her, but he also remembered losing his wife in a terrible accident with this same horse. "I don't know, Lily. I just don't know."

Astra chose that moment to flail her legs and grunt loudly. Lily took two steps, intent on running back to her side, but Dr. Tison put a hand on her shoulder and held her back.

"Not so fast, Lily," Dr. Tison warned. "She could accidentally strike you with those front legs if she does that again."

"The doc is right," Lily's father said. "And this proves my point about the danger of you getting hurt."

Lily crossed her arms. "That's *so* unfair!" she protested. "I could get hurt riding my bike to the store. I could get hurt walking to the school bus. I could get hurt during gym class at school." She clamped her lips shut, knowing she'd gone too far, but she was unable to stop herself. She'd managed to holler at every adult there and double the load of worry for her father. Not only was she going to lose Astra, but she was going to be in major trouble later. And she deserved it. Lily hung her head, knowing she'd lost the battle. Would it do any good to throw herself at Mr. Henley's feet and beg him to let Astra live?

Mr. O'Neil sighed. "Give me a few days to get a stall ready at our place," he said to the ranch owner.

Lily's head snapped up in surprise. Did her father just say...*yes?*

Mr. O'Neil turned to Lily. "I expect you to keep up your end of the bargain. You'll be here to help Steven for a few hours after school when he needs you, and on the weekends. And the no-riding rule is still in effect."

Lily nodded her head vigorously. She felt like one of those bobblehead dolls she'd seen on car dashboards. "I promise!" she said. She ran to her father, threw her arms around him, and hugged him tight. "Thank you, thank you, thank you!" she exclaimed.

"Well, finish up here and call me when you're ready to come home," Mr. O'Neil said with a small smile. "You've got school tomorrow. Astra is in good hands here."

Lily gave her dad one last squeeze and ran back to Astra's side. The beautiful Arabian mare was hers. Really and truly hers!

Eight

ily spent the next afternoon helping Dr. Tison care for Astra. The mare was awake, but very weak. By eight o'clock that evening, when her dad insisted she come home, the vet declared that Astra would make it through the night. Lily felt horrible having to leave her, but she had confidence in Dr. Tison's diagnosis.

Two important battles had been won today: Astra had survived and Lily's dad had agreed to let her keep the mare. *A double miracle,* she thought as she watched Dr. Tison work.

A car horn sounded outside the barn.

"There's your ride," Dr. Tison said. He removed the last IV bottle and helped Astra roll into an upright position with her legs tucked under her. "Congratulations, Lily. I'm not sure how things are going to work out for you and this horse, but you saved her life today. Your mother would be very proud."

Lily smiled broadly. "*We* saved her life today, Dr. Tison. It took both of us." She shoved her hands deep into her pockets and stared at the ground. "I don't know how I'm ever going to pay you back for all this." She nodded toward Astra. "I'll work hard, and it might take me until I'm twenty, but I'll get it done."

The vet laughed. "How about if you start by calling me Dr. Dale? That's what your mother used to do. After everything we've gone through today, I think we can do with a little less formality."

Lily grinned. "Okay, Dr. Dale."

The vet finished with Astra and let himself out of the stall. "I meant what I told your father earlier, Lily. I'll donate today's vet work, and the medication she'll need in the coming weeks."

"I can't let you do that," Lily protested. She also knew her father's pride wouldn't allow him to accept so much charity. "We had a vet come to our school to talk on Career Day. He told us about all the school loans he had to take out to get his degree, and that it would take him forever to pay them back."

The vet chuckled. "Sounds like he wanted to scare you kids off," he said, "instead of encouraging you to go into veterinary medicine."

The car horn sounded again. This time it was a double beep.

"Better get going," Dr. Dale said. "Don't worry about the money, Lily. This one horse won't break me. But I want you to make me a promise."

Lily listened intently. The vet's serious tone told her that this was important.

"In the next few days, we'll be doing more blood tests on Astra to see how all her organs are functioning," Dr. Dale went on. "If the tests come back saying she has permanent liver damage, or something equally bad, you need to promise that you'll let me put her to sleep—no matter how much you love her. I know it hurts to lose a pet you love, but there comes a time when you need to think of the animal's welfare and what's best for them."

He put a comforting hand on her shoulder and steered her toward the barn door. "It's the adult thing to do, and it's the right thing to do. Do you understand me on this?"

Lily kept her head down, but nodded. She didn't really want to think about it, but she realized she might have to in the near future. "I promise," Lily said, swallowing hard.

"Get a good night's sleep," the vet said as he waved to her father in the pickup truck. "We'll take good care of Astra and she'll be here waiting for you in the morning."

The short ride home was quiet. Lily had the feeling her dad already regretted his decision to let her keep Astra. When she got home, she quickly laid out her clothes for school, then brushed her teeth and prepared for bed. She didn't want to give her father a chance to back out of the deal, so she quickly kissed him and her grandmother good night and went to bed.

Falling asleep was difficult with all the events of the day rolling around in her head, but eventually exhaustion won out and Lily drifted into a deep slumber.

* * *

She woke with a start when Grams tapped on the bedroom door the next morning. Lily looked at the clock sleepily. The bus would arrive in fifteen minutes! She must have shut off the alarm. She bounded out of bed, got dressed in record time, and rushed down to the kitchen.

Her first thought was Astra, but her father had other ideas. "Absolutely not, Lily, we can't stop by Henley's ranch and check on Astra. There's no time," he said as he gathered his lunch bucket and jacket. "Someone would have called if something were wrong. Why don't you call them while I warm the truck up?"

Lily reached for the phone. If Charlie and Jill rode the school bus, she could have asked them in person, but they went to a private school, and their dad always drove them there. She dialed the barn number and Thomas picked it up on the third ring. She sighed in relief when the stable manager told her that Astra was hanging in there. Dr. Tison even thought she was improving a bit.

"Thanks, Thomas." Lily hung up the phone with a smile and grabbed her things for school. Her hair was a mess, she hadn't eaten breakfast, and she wasn't sure her clothes matched, but it didn't matter. Astra had survived the night— and she was getting better!

Lily's dad swung the door open as she raced toward the truck. "I can tell by the big grin that the news must have been good."

Lily nodded and slid into the seat, watching her breath frost the inside of the cab. The weatherman on the truck's radio said a warming trend was approaching. She sure hoped so. It seemed like winter had gone on forever, and she was ready for some warm breezes. Sunshine and warmth would help Astra, too.

"Thomas said Astra is improving." Lily reached over and flipped through the stations until she found one that she knew both she and her father could agree on.

"That's good," he said, but Lily could see his knuckles tighten on the steering wheel.

She reached out and touched his sleeve. "Dad, I know this is going to be hard on you. But I think this is what mom would have wanted. I really do." She watched her father force a smile to his lips. It looked rather pained, but at least he was trying.

They came to the end of the long dirt road and Lily was surprised to see someone sitting at her bus stop. There were several ranch kids at the stop before hers and a few at the next, but Lily and Meloney were the only kids who used this one. She knew Mel wouldn't be there today because she had said something about an early dentist appointment. But now, a boy about her age with shaggy blond hair was waiting on the bench, looking a bit lost.

Lily and Meloney usually sat in the truck with her dad until the bus arrived, but she felt kind of silly sitting in the warm truck staring at the boy, who was probably pretty uncomfortable on the cold bench.

"Should we invite him in here where it's warm?" Mr. O'Neil asked. "He must be from the family that moved into the old ranch down the way. "

Lily observed the new boy. He was lean, with high cheekbones and a cute face. Actually, he was very cute. Her face grew warm at the thought and her hand went to her tangled hair. *Yikes.*

She wished her dad would drive her all the way to school. Then she could start again tomorrow with brushed hair and a better pair of jeans. But she knew that wouldn't happen. His job was in the opposite direction from the school. "That's okay, Dad. I'll go out and sit on the bench with him."

"All right, if you insist." Her father gave her a peck on the cheek. "I'll still wait here until the bus comes."

Great, Lily thought. Her dad was going to sit there and watch her struggle through uncomfortable conversation with the new boy. She reached down for her backpack and cringed when she noticed her mismatched socks.

She managed to get out of the truck without falling on her face. The boy nodded his head politely and moved over on the bench to make room. Lily thought about her unmatched socks and decided to stand. She didn't want them peeking out if her jeans rode up when she sat. "Hi, my name is Lily," she said. Immediately she felt like a dork.

"I'm Devin," the boy said as he shoved his hands deep into his jacket pockets. "My family just moved into the big tan house down the road." He grinned. "We're from southern California so I'm not used to this cold weather."

Devin seemed friendly as well as cute. Lily dropped her backpack at her feet and pulled on her gloves. "Yeah, it gets kind of cold here in the winter, but the weather's supposed to warm up soon. Spring's always pretty nice here up North."

The sound of the bus chugging up the hill saved Lily from any more conversation. At least now she wouldn't have to worry about making a fool of herself by saying something totally stupid. She turned and waved to her dad, then waited for the bus to come to a complete stop. The bus driver smiled as she stepped onboard. Lily took a seat three rows back while the driver motioned for Devin to sit up front. She wanted to give him the no-monkey-business-on-my-bus speech.

When they reached the school, Lily braced herself for what she knew would be the longest day of the year. All she wanted to do was get home and see Astra, but she had a lot of classes to get through before she could do that. She tightened her grip on the strap of her backpack. The sooner she started, the quicker she'd get home.

* * *

No amount of clock watching would make time move faster. After what seemed like a twenty-four-hour school day, Lily finally stepped off the bus and into her grandmother's car. Devin hadn't taken the bus home, and she hadn't seen him in class. Lily thought he might be a grade or two ahead of her. She pulled off her gloves and settled her backpack at her feet.

The weather had warmed to fifty-five degrees. She decided it would be a perfect time to start working on Astra's stall and paddock. But first she wanted to get to the Henleys' as fast as possible and see her horse.

Her horse.

She loved the sound of those words. Her mother would be so excited for her. "Grams, can we go straight to the barn, please? I want to see Astra."

Her grandmother smiled. "I would've been surprised if you'd wanted to go anyplace else."

Lily sat back in her seat and put on her seat belt. "You're the best, Grams."

Her grandmother glanced into the rearview mirror and pulled onto the road. "Yes, dear, I know."

Mr. Henley was standing in the driveway, holding a horse for the shoer, when they got to the ranch. "You just missed Dr. Tison," he said. "But he gave Astra good marks. Says she's getting stronger."

Charlie came out through the barn door with a loaded wheelbarrow. "Hi, Silly Lily. Dr. Tison says Astra might be able to stand by tomorrow."

Silly Lily? That was even dumber than Lil-pill. Lily shook her head. Some things never changed. Charlie would always be a bonehead. But at least he had good news.

She helped her grandmother down the aisle, guiding her along to Astra's stall. "Hiya, girl," she said as she opened the stall door and knelt beside the gray mare. It was so amazing to see her respond by flicking her ears and reaching her nose out to touch her shirtfront.

"Isn't she beautiful?" Lily said to Grams proudly. "I'm going to go home and build her a nice pen and a stall so she can live with us as soon as she's strong enough to walk."

Gram raised her eyebrows. "Really?" was all she said.

Lily hung around and fussed over the mare for a few more minutes. Then she and her grandmother hurried home so Lily could get started on her project.

"Honey, have you ever built a fence before?" Grams asked when they pulled into the driveway.

Lily got out of the car and walked with her grandmother into the house. "No, but I've seen Thomas fix fences at Whispering Pines. It didn't look that hard." She frowned at the knowing chuckle her grandmother tried to cover up.

"Maybe you should wait for your father," Grams suggested. "He did say he'd fix her a stall."

"He'll get home too late," Lily said. "I've only got a few more hours of daylight left and I don't want to wait. Besides, he doesn't really like Astra. It'll be better if I do it." She kicked off her shoes and went to her room to change. Old, torn jeans and a ratty sweatshirt were the order of the day. She didn't want to damage her good clothes by catching them on a nail and ripping them.

The sun felt warm on Lily's cheeks as she stepped off her back porch and walked toward the old barn. It had been a while since she'd visited the place. Memories of her beloved pony still lingered in the empty structure. Ever since her father had torn up the fences and taken down the walls of most of the stalls to make room for equipment, she'd been avoiding it.

She threw the barn doors wide, letting in the light so she could see what was still usable. The stall on the end was still intact, with only a few boards missing. And the paddock off the stall had escaped her father's destruction derby when he was making room for his equipment. There were a lot of boards missing from the fence line, and a post or two that looked questionable, but all in all, if she could make the repairs, Astra would have a good home.

She smiled when she thought about the beautiful Arabian mare coming to live with them. She could have stood there and daydreamed about it for hours, but she had a fence to build and limited hours of daylight.

Peering inside her dad's toolshed, Lily had her first inkling of doubt. The shed held many tools, most of which she couldn't even name, let alone figure out how to use. But all she needed were a hammer and nails.

She found her dad's tool belt and strapped it around her waist. It had pockets for nails and a place to hold a hammer. After a little more digging, she found a box of two-inch nails and the hammer. With a few boards off the woodpile she'd be in business.

Lily stepped out the door, feeling pretty proud of herself. Her grandmother might have doubts about her ability to build a fence, but Lily felt sure she could do it. After all, it was just a matter of nailing up a few boards, right?

Nine

Okay, so maybe fence building wasn't as easy as she'd thought. Lily stood back and surveyed her work. She'd only nailed on a few boards, but they were hopelessly crooked and the nails kept bending. She wiped her hand across her cheek, trying to push back the stray hairs that stuck to her face. She looked at the pile of boards still waiting for her to hammer them on. Maybe she should have waited for her dad.

The sound of a whinnying horse broke the silence. Lily cocked her head, trying to determine where it had come from. The thud of hoofbeats seemed to be approaching from her left. She gazed down the narrow trail that ran behind their house.

A boy trotted down the path on a beautiful black horse with a big white star in the center of its forehead. As they drew closer, Lily could see that the horse was an Arabian. Its dished face, fine muzzle, and long elegant neck showed the horse's fine breeding.

Lily moved closer to the fence to get a better look. The horse moved out with long, sweeping strides and the rider posted in perfect time to the gait. All thoughts of fence construction disappeared as Lily lost herself in the sight of a horse and rider in perfect harmony.

It wasn't until they trotted past that Lily recognized the boy as the new kid, Devin, from the bus stop. That was a surprise. He hadn't seemed like a horse person, somehow.

"Whoa." Devin pulled his mount to a halt and turned around.

Lily stiffened. Was he coming back to speak to her? A freeze-frame image of what she looked like right now flitted across her brain: baggy pants, ratty sweatshirt, dirt and cobwebs all over her clothing. And her hair was a total mess. She never cared what Charlie thought about her. But she didn't want this new boy to think she was a total loser. She'd looked bad enough this morning.

"Hey, it's Lily, right?" The boy pulled his horse to a stop in front of her and smiled.

Lily nodded. The black horse poked his nose toward her and she stroked his soft muzzle. "He's beautiful," she said. "What's his name?"

"Jericho." Devin leaned down and patted the gelding's neck. "We've got twelve races under our saddle in southern California. I'm hoping to find some good races here this summer. I'm figuring, since this is the home of the Tevis Cup, that there must be a bunch of smaller races in this area."

Lily perked up. Here was something she could talk about and not feel dumb. "Mr. Henley owns a big Arabian ranch down the road. He's got a nationally qualified endurance mare and a stable full of racers. My friend, Meloney, competes in the fifty-mile races, too."

Devin stepped off his horse and pulled Jericho's reins over his head. Lily gulped. It looked like the boy planned to stay and talk for a while. She wasn't very good at talking to people she didn't know that well—especially boys.

Devin stared at the hammer in her hands and the work belt cinched around her waist. "Building a fence?" He looked at the rickety boards with his brows raised and then back to her.

The fence looked so pathetic, Lily thought about fibbing, but her parents had taught her that the truth was always best. And she couldn't exactly deny the hammer and nails she held in her hands. "I, um, thought I could do it by myself." She shrugged. "But I guess I don't know what I'm doing."

Devin stepped Jericho over the broken fence. "Let me find a place to put him and I'll help you."

"Really?" Lily was caught by surprise. "But aren't you taking your horse out for a ride?"

Devin grinned. "The trail will still be there tomorrow. Right now it looks like you could use some help."

"You can put Jericho in our backyard to graze," Lily offered. "I'll get another hammer." She ran back to her father's toolshed and got another hammer and more nails. Devin was already pulling broken boards off the fence when she returned.

"Looks like we could replace maybe ten boards and the pen will be good enough to hold an animal." Devin brushed his blond hair out of his eyes and looked around.

Green. His eyes were green. Lily had expected them to be blue.

"I don't see any horses or cows," Devin said. "What do you plan to put in here?"

"Huh?" Lily realized she'd been staring and not really paying attention. After he repeated the question, she handed Devin his tool belt and the nails. "It's a long story," she said. Quickly, she told Devin the short version of the story while she helped him pull the rest of the broken boards off the posts.

"Wow," Devin said. "Sorry about your mom. That's really sad. But that's pretty cool about Astra. I can't believe someone gave you a horse—especially one your mom thought could be a champion."

Grams stuck her head out the back door and hollered, "Lily, your friend is here!" She saw the black gelding grazing in the backyard and stepped onto the porch. "Whose horse is this?"

Lily motioned for Devin to step around the side of the barn. "Grams, this is Devin. His family just moved into the valley and he goes to my school. He rode by on his horse and stopped to help me fix the fence."

Meloney came around the corner in time to hear the introduction. She lifted a curious eyebrow and silently mouthed *cute* behind Devin's back. Lily felt her cheeks grow warm.

"What a nice young man," Grams said. "Thank you, Devin. And now that there are three of you, I bet you can get that fence fixed in no time. I'll make some snacks and bring them out in a bit."

Lily found an extra pair of gloves for Meloney, and with Devin's fence-building skills, the job went quickly. They even patched up the stall. Just as they finished putting the tools away, Grams came out with a plate of small sandwiches.

"Awesome. Thanks!" Devin said as he grabbed a sandwich and stuffed it in his mouth.

Melony and Lily each reached for three sandwiches.

"You eat like a girl on a diet," Meloney teased Devin.

He blushed and took a couple more of the little sandwiches. "I was just trying to be polite."

"Just don't tell your father I wrecked your appetite, Lily," her grandmother laughed. "You'd better eat all your dinner or I'll be in trouble."

Devin took one more sandwich, then went to bridle his horse. "Thanks again, Mrs. O'Neil." He led his horse from the yard and mounted up. He looked back at Lily and Meloney. "Guess I'll see you guys at school tomorrow?"

"Guess so. And thanks a lot for your help," Lily said. "You, too, Meloney. I couldn't have done it without you guys."

"Sure you could have," Devin said. "I bet it would have been an interesting fence, too." He grinned as he wheeled his horse and cantered off.

"Nice guy," Meloney said. "Plus he's a serious endurance rider. It's going to be a lot more fun riding with him than pain-in-the-neck Charlie."

Lily felt a twinge of jealousy. "For you, maybe."

"I'm sorry, Lily. But hey, you've got a horse now, after your dad said you could never have another one. Who knows? Maybe someday soon you'll be able to ride again, too."

Lily's grandmother grabbed the empty sandwich tray and headed into the house. "I didn't hear anything you just said, Miss Meloney. So I can ignore everything that I *didn't* hear."

The girls laughed as they walked to the front of the house to get Meloney's bike.

"Your grandma's great," Meloney said. She picked up her bike and pointed it for home. "Call and let me know how Astra is doing after you go see her tonight."

"I will," Lily promised. She waved good-bye to her friend and went into the house to wash up, just as her father's truck pulled into the driveway. She hoped he'd be happy about the work they'd done on the fence and stall. Maybe even happy enough to take her over to see Astra after dinner.

* * *

"Slow down, Lily," her father scolded as she ran down the barn aisle.

Thomas stepped from the tack room. "Lily, wait a minute. I've got something to show you and I think you're going to be really surprised."

Lily and her father fell into step behind Thomas. He led them to Astra's stall and opened the door. Lily gasped. Astra was standing in the middle of her stall. The mare nickered when she saw Lily. She ran to the mare and threw her arms around her neck. "You're better!" Lily cried, burying her nose in Astra's mane.

Mr. O'Neil shifted from foot to foot and frowned. "Maybe you shouldn't be in there, Lily?"

Thomas waved him off. "It's her horse now, and Astra loves her. Some extra attention from Lily is just what this mare needs."

Mr. O'Neil did not look convinced.

"So is she completely okay now?" Lily asked.

"She's very weak," Thomas said, "but she wanted to stand a little while ago, so Steven and I helped her up. She's shuffled around a bit and eaten a few wisps of hay." He offered the mare a handful of grass hay and Astra lipped a few strands from his palm. "All of these are very good signs, but she's a long way from being well. Dr. Tison took another blood sample earlier. He'll compare it to the one he took this morning and see if anything has changed."

Lily planted a kiss on the mare's soft muzzle. "Can I make her a hot bran mash? Won't that help make her stronger?"

Thomas shook his head. "Doc's orders. Nothing but plain ol' grass hay for the first twenty-four hours. When she's eating with a healthy appetite, we can try her on something with a little more protein content."

Lily picked the bedding out of Astra's mane and finger-combed some of the tangles. "We fixed you a stall and pen today," Lily told the mare. "As soon as you're strong enough, we can move you over to our house."

She glanced over and saw another frown on her father's face. Lily tried to ignore it, but his disapproval nagged at her. He'd told her she could keep Astra, and she was so close to bringing the mare home. Astra needed to gain strength quickly before her father changed his mind.

Ten

The rest of the week passed in a blur. Lily spent every school day watching the clock. She hurried home to finish her homework, and then she was off to the barn to spend the rest of the day with Astra. She brushed the mare, picked her hooves, and made sure she had plenty of fresh hay and water. Dr. Dale had given the okay to start Astra back on warm bran mash with a small amount of rolled oats. Her appetite was almost back to normal, and Lily had even begun taking her on small walks.

On Friday, Lily finished her homework early and rode her bike down to the Henley barn. She'd just started feeding Astra when Charlie appeared. He hung around the stall, trying to bother Lily, but her spirits were too high to let him bring her down. "Have you met the new kid yet?" she asked. "His name is Devin and he's got a really nice endurance horse. He plans to ride in the races this year."

Charlie shrugged. "I talked to him a little. I've heard he's an okay rider, but I'm not afraid of competition. My dad's got Derringer, the new gelding that he thinks is going to be really good. He's going to let me ride him this season." He handed Lily a hay net full of good grass hay. "I looked up the stats on Devin's gelding. Derringer will blow him right off the trail."

Lily chuckled to herself as she hung the hay net in the corner. If Charlie wasn't worried, he wouldn't have looked up Jericho's stats. It would be a lot of fun to ride the races with everybody this year and watch the sparks fly. Meloney was so lucky.

Mr. Henley stopped by the stall. "Well, Lily, if you're still serious about working for me, you can start this weekend."

"Great!" Lily said. She needed to make money right away to pay for Astra's feed.

"And the good news is, Dr. Tison said Astra is strong enough to move to your house. After you finish work tomorrow, you can take her home."

"All right!" Lily even slapped Charlie a high five. "I can't believe it!" She threw her arms around the mare's neck and hugged her tight. Astra snorted at the sudden movement and Lily smiled. Arabians were very high-strung. That simple snort told her that the mare was definitely on the mend. She couldn't wait to get her home.

* * *

That night at the dinner table, Lily decided it might be a good idea if she told her dad that Astra would be arriving the following day.

"Are you sure you can take care of her?" her father asked when she gave him the news. "An Arabian is a lot different than a pony. Astra won't have the same temperament as Domino."

"Now, Daniel," Grams said, passing him the mashed potatoes and motioning for the salad bowl. "Katherine spent a lot of time making sure Lily knew how to handle horses. Your wife knew what she was doing. She taught her daughter well."

Lily's father paused with the bowl in midair. "Yes, Katherine knew what she was doing. She was a pro. And she still…" He put down the bowl and frowned.

The table got very quiet. Lily looked from her father to her grandmother. She took a deep breath. "Go ahead and say it, Dad."

Her father shook his head, refusing to look at her.

Lily tried to keep her voice strong and steady. "Please, Dad. Go ahead."

Her father's jaw tightened. "Forget I said anything. Let's eat."

Lily picked up her fork and gathered her courage. "Then I'll say it. Mom knew what she was doing, *but she died anyway*. There. I said it. It's out in the open." She shoved a huge bite of casserole into her mouth, hoping that she wouldn't get sent to her room for sassing her father. She shouldn't have done it. But her mother's death hung heavily over the entire household. It needed to be brought out in the open.

Mr. O'Neil sighed loudly. "You're right, Lily. It's out there. And losing you is my biggest fear. You're just going to have to bear with me while I try to get used to this new arrangement. I lost your mother, and I cannot bear the thought of losing you, too."

"We're going to get through this, Dad. I'll be safe, I promise." Lily got out of her chair and walked around the table to give her dad a big hug. "Everything will work out fine. You just wait and see."

* * *

Lily hardly slept a wink that night. She rose before the alarm the next morning and made it to the barn ahead of schedule. Thomas was just putting on the coffeepot. She went to say hello to her horse, then returned to the tack room to make herself a hot chocolate.

"Today's the big day, right?" Thomas said. He poured himself a mug of the strong brew and made a face as he swallowed. "You finally get to take that mare home. I'm really happy things are working out, Lily." He put down the coffee mug. "And you know, to tell you the truth, I don't think the same way Mr. Henley does. I don't believe Astra is all washed up."

"You don't?" Lily raised her eyebrows.

Thomas shook his head. "That mare was at death's door and I know she's going to have some problems going forward. But a few months from now, if you take really good care of her, Astra may bounce back and be just fine. Dr. Tison feels that's a possibility."

Lily's pulse quickened. "You mean…she could be rideable again?"

Thomas shrugged. "If all of her insides go back to functioning correctly, and her blood work comes back good, why not?" He handed Lily a stack of buckets for the morning grain. "I'm not saying she'll ever be a racer again—but I'm also not willing to say she won't."

Lily took the buckets to the grain bin and measured out rations for the first six horses. Astra stuck her head over her stall door and banged on the wooden panel, neighing for her grain with the rest of them. Lily couldn't help but smile. Another good sign.

Charlie showed up twenty minutes later, just as Lily and Thomas finished graining the horses. "Hey, Lily, guess who's coming over to ride with me today?"

Lily already knew that Meloney would be there. She rode with the Henleys every chance she could and rarely missed a Saturday.

"Devin," Charlie announced before she could guess. "Jill told him we'd show him our training trails."

Lily wasn't sure why, but she felt a small twisting inside when she thought about Jill showing Devin all the great riding trails. She wished she could be the one out there, enjoying the fresh air, great scenery, and an awesome horse trotting down the trail under her saddle.

Maybe someday, if Astra got better.... Quickly she dismissed that thought. At this point her dad would ground her for even thinking about riding the mare. But Thomas thought it a possibility and so did Dr. Dale.

"Lily?" Mr. Henley's voice echoed down the barn aisle. "We need to get these horses saddled as soon as they're finished with their grain. We've got a long ride today and company coming to join us. If you saddle Contina, I'll get Charlie's new horse ready."

"You got it, Mr. Henley," Lily said. She held out the halter and Contina put her nose into it. The talented mare was a half sister to Astra and they shared many similar traits. This year, Contina would race in the Tevis Cup, and Mr. Henley hoped to finish in the Top Ten. Lily bit her lip. Too bad Astra would probably never have a chance to compete in the Tevis with her sister. Or any other race, for that matter.

A commotion sounded at the end of the barn aisle. Lily glanced up to see Mr. Henley walking a magnificent chestnut with four white socks and a blaze down the aisle. The gelding snorted and pranced, poking his nose at every horse that stuck its head over the stall door.

That must be Derringer, Lily thought as she snapped Contina into the cross ties. She'd heard talk around the barn of the new horse the Henleys had purchased, in addition to Charlie's bragging. The spirited gelding must have been delivered after she left the barn last night.

Mr. Henley brought the chestnut next to Contina. The younger horse flexed his neck and threatened to bite her.

"Hey!" Lily cried, taking a swat at the badly behaved gelding's nose. The chestnut snorted at the reprimand, but he moved over and quit making threatening gestures.

"Don't touch my horse," Charlie said. "He was only playing. Derringer is going to be a great racer and I don't want to break his spirit."

Lily frowned in annoyance. She opened her mouth to tell Charlie what she thought of his ill-mannered horse, but Mr. Henley cut her off.

"Lily was right to correct him," Mr. Henley said, as he removed his knit hat from the horse's lips. "This gelding is too full of himself. All he wants to do is play. We need to keep better control of him. He loves people, but he acts like a big, playful puppy dog. We need to remember he's a horse and show him how to behave. I don't want anyone getting hurt."

Jill entered the barn, dressed in a new pair of expensive leather paddock boots, gray riding breeches, and a stylish winter jacket she'd bought on a shopping trip to San Francisco. Lily couldn't help being jealous of the girl. There was no way her own family could ever afford to buy her riding gear like that. She looked down at her own faded jeans. Devin was going to see her looking like a bum again.

"Meloney and Devin are coming up the road," Jill said. She grabbed her saddle and a brush box from the tack room and headed toward her horse's stall.

Lily sighed. Meloney was so lucky, too. Then Contina

shoved her with her nose and Lily remembered that she was supposed to be saddling the mare, not envying her friends. By the time she got Contina tacked and walked her out the barn door, Meloney and Devin were just stepping into the stable yard.

"Hi, Lily." Devin waved from atop Jericho's back. "What's up?"

Lily couldn't help grinning. "I get to take Astra home today."

"That's awesome!" Meloney said.

"Great news," Devin agreed.

Charlie walked Derringer from the barn and strapped on his riding helmet.

"Wow, nice horse," Devin said. Jericho nickered and extended his muzzle toward the flashy chestnut. Derringer greeted him with a quick nip on the end of his soft nose. "Hey, watch it!" Devin immediately backed Jericho up several steps.

"Aw, he's just playing. He didn't mean anything by it." Charlie stuck his foot into the stirrup and mounted up. Derringer took several steps to the side and snorted. Charlie patted the gelding's neck. "He's just excited and ready to hit the trail. Good luck keeping up with us, Devin," he called over his shoulder as he jogged the colt in a big circle to get his mind on business.

Jill walked her mare from the barn and mounted up. "This isn't a race, Charlie. Save the smack talk for the real thing. We're just going for a training ride and showing Devin the trails today."

Lily waited for Mr. Henley to come collect his mare so she could get on with her chores. She wanted this day to be over

78

so she could take Astra home. Plus, she felt out of place standing there on foot while the others sat atop their beautiful endurance horses.

Meloney moved her horse next to Contina and leaned down to speak to Lily. "I'll help you take Astra home when we get back from our ride. I'll cool Jasper out here and clean him up while you're finishing your work. Then we can pony her back to your house on Jasper if you want."

"That would be really great." Lily smiled at her friend.

"I'll help, too," Devin offered. "I'd like to be there when you turn her loose in that amazing pen we built."

Lily thought about all the mismatched boards and bent nails on their fence. They must have all been thinking the same thing because they burst out laughing at the same time.

"What's so funny?" Charlie asked, riding up.

Lily thought about explaining, but decided it would be more fun to keep it as her and Meloney and Devin's little secret. Mr. Henley showed up right then and saved her from having to answer any of Charlie's questions.

"Thank you, Lily." Mr. Henley took the reins and mounted up. "We'll be back in about four hours. Thomas has a list of things for you to do while we're gone. When we get back, we'll see about getting Astra ready to go to her new home." He winked and reined his mare in a half circle, motioning for the rest of them to follow him down the driveway.

Devin gave her a snappy salute as he trotted off. Meloney and Jill waved.

"See you later, Lil-Pill!" Charlie hollered as he squeezed his calves against Derringer's sides and moved off to join them. Derringer gave a little crow hop and Charlie pulled the gelding alongside Jericho.

He kept his horse nose to nose with Jericho. Even from where she stood, Lily could tell Charlie was watching Devin closely.

Lily had the feeling she was witnessing the beginning of a big rivalry—and it wasn't going to be a friendly one.

Eleven

Astra stepped into the deep straw bedding of her new stall and snorted. The Henleys bedded their stalls with shavings, but Astra seemed to like the golden straw. She pawed at it, then lowered her head and nibbled at some of the smaller stems.

"I think she likes it," Lily said.

Devin and Meloney nodded in agreement.

Lily's dad stood a few steps behind them with his hands in his pockets and a solemn look on his face.

Grams leaned over the stall door and offered Astra a piece of apple. The mare lifted her head, her nostrils flared to inhale the scent. When she recognized it, she stepped forward and accepted the treat, crunching the crisp apple and looking for more. "I think it's good to have a horse back in this barn again," Grams said.

Lily smiled so big her cheeks hurt. No doubt about it, having Astra here in their very own barn was wonderful!

"Okay, ladies, let's head in for dinner," Mr. O'Neil said. "Astra has had enough attention for the night. Lily, say goodbye to your friends and come wash up for dinner."

"Okay, Dad."

Devin waited until the adults were gone before he spoke. "I don't think your dad is very happy about having Astra around."

"Are you sure everything's going to be okay?" Meloney asked. "If he gets too weird about it, you can always bring Astra over to my house."

"Thanks, Mel," Lily said. "I hope it doesn't come to that, but you're right. My dad doesn't seem to be getting used to this whole horse-owning idea. Maybe he'll change his mind once he sees what a great horse Astra is."

Devin untied Jericho from the hitching post. "Just be safe and play by his rules. Your dad's worried about you getting hurt, that's all." He shrugged. "You can't really blame him after everything that happened with your mom. You'll have to prove to him that you can be safe. Then maybe he'll get off your back about it."

Lily knew Devin was right. But she *was* following the rules. What more could she do to ease her father's mind?

After Meloney and Devin had left, she headed into the house, breathing in the wonderful aromas of herb-roasted chicken, fresh-baked bread, and maybe, if her nose was right, a chocolate pie. Her grandmother was the best! Lily took her seat at the table.

"Your cheeks certainly are rosy," Grams said as she passed the platter of chicken. "And that's the most sparkle I've seen in those eyes in a long time." She turned to her son. "You made the right decision in letting Lily keep the horse, Daniel."

Lily's father grunted and took a big bite of his chicken. Lily wished he could be happy for her. She knew he was trying, but she wished he would try a bit harder. "The weather is getting warmer," Lily said. "I saw some new grass popping up. Dad, could you please help me fix that little pasture where Domino used to graze?"

Her father hesitated so long Lily feared he might say no. She saw her grandma shift in her chair, as if she were about to kick him in the shins under the table.

"Sure, Lily. Come get me as soon as you finish your work for the Henleys tomorrow. I'll probably be out in the barn, working on the old lawn mower."

"Thanks, Dad. I should be home by one o'clock." Lily smiled. Her father agreeing to help her with horse stuff when she knew he didn't really want to was an encouraging sign.

Mr. O'Neil placed another chicken leg on Lily's plate. "Better eat up, Flower. You're going to need your strength if we're fixing fence on the lower field tomorrow. It may take a little more energy to get the boards on straight this time."

Lily laughed. Her dad was definitely trying, and she loved him for it.

* * *

Over the next several weeks, Astra picked up in appetite and strength. The proud Arabian also grew in spirit. Sometimes it was all Lily could do to get the mare from her stall and out to the small pasture without her breaking away.

Dr. Dale came for weekly check-ups on the horse, each time proclaiming he couldn't believe how quickly Astra had recovered—or that she had recovered at all.

"This is a miracle mare," Dr. Dale said when Astra's latest blood test showed she was almost back to normal. "I think you can start a light exercise program with her. Just make sure you start out slow and easy and work your way up."

Lily smiled. She wasn't sure Astra could do anything slow

or easy. "Good," she said. "Because she's about ready to pull my arm out of the socket every time I take her out of the stall." *Too bad I can't ride her down the road for some exercise,* Lily added to herself. She pressed her cheek against Astra's neck and breathed in the wonderful warm horse smell, then sighed in exasperation. How was she ever going to keep from riding the beautiful Arabian mare when she was right here under her barn roof? But a promise was a promise.

* * *

At the end of March, when the grass began to turn green and tulips poked their heads through the soil, Lily started Astra on a longeing program. She began by attaching the twenty-five-foot longe line to Astra's halter and asking the mare to trot in a circle around her. Lily did this for a couple of minutes at a time while Astra's strength improved. Soon Lily worked the mare up to fifteen minutes of trotting. Longeing didn't seem to be enough to take the extra energy out of her.

Lily released Astra into her small pasture. The mare tore around the corral with her gray tail over her back, snorting and kicking up her heels. She ran several laps, then came to a sliding halt and stared over the fence with her ears pricked, gazing into the distance.

What is she looking at? Lily wondered. Then, suddenly, she knew. "You miss racing, don't you, girl? You want to be out there on the trails with your friends." Lily stood still, staring in the same direction as her horse. She wished she could be out there, too.

* * *

The next day, Mel and Devin stopped by to see how Astra was doing.

"She looks great," Devin said.

"Yeah," Meloney agreed. "Just think, it was only a month ago that Mr. Henley thought Astra was a goner. Who knew she'd bounce back this quickly?"

Lily shivered at the thought of how close she'd come to losing the proud Arabian.

"Yeah, she's pretty amazing." Lily held out her hand and Astra trotted to the center of the pen where her owner stood. "Good girl," Lily crooned, patting the mare's long arched neck. She looked back at her friends, who were sitting on the top rail of the fence. "I'm not sure where to go from here," she admitted. "My dad won't let me ride, but I can't just keep running Astra in circles. Too much of that would be bad for her joints. I've got to do something, though, because she sure is getting restless. Longeing isn't enough for her anymore."

"How about ponying her?" Devin suggested.

"Yeah, she did okay when we were bringing her home from the Henleys," Meloney said.

Lily thought for a minute. Ponying meant that a rider rode one horse and led another. It was a good way of getting some serious exercise into a horse without him carrying a rider. Or, if a trainer was breaking a new horse to ride and didn't trust him on his own, the trainer could pony the new horse and rider so there would be less chance of the rider getting bucked off.

"My mom used to do that with me and my old pony, Domino," Lily said. "When we first got him, he could be a bit of a handful. My mom would pony us down that long stretch of road. By the time we turned for home, he was usually tired enough that I could handle him on my own." She chuckled at the memory, but it made her a little sad, too.

"Do you want to try it with Astra?" Devin offered. "I'm pretty good at ponying."

A door banged shut at the front of the O'Neil house and Astra suddenly spun on her heels, kicking up sand as she raced around the paddock, snorting and tossing her head.

"Wooo, look at her go!" Meloney hollered. "That horse definitely needs some more exercise. I think you better take Devin up on his offer, Lily."

"Sure." Devin climbed down from the fence. "I'll bring Jericho by after school tomorrow and we can give it a try," he said. "Right now, though, I've got to get home. If I'm late for dinner, my mom will give me extra chores."

"Sounds like a plan," Lily told him. "Thanks."

She called Astra to her side and snapped the lead shank on her royal blue halter. She couldn't wait until tomorrow!

* * *

"Why the big rush?" Mr. O'Neil asked when Lily jumped into the old truck after school the next day and waved good-bye to her friends at the bus stop.

Lily dumped her book bag on the floor and latched her seat belt. "Devin and Meloney are coming over to pony Astra today. I need to make sure she's brushed and ready."

Her father glanced across the seat at her. "Your mom used to do that sometimes when she was getting horses ready to race and she didn't have time to ride them both. Are you thinking about training Astra for one of your friends to race?"

Lily looked up in surprise. "No, Dad. Astra just has a lot of energy now that she's feeling better, and I can't ride her...I thought maybe if I could just—"

She saw the immediate frown on her father's face. "Lily," he cut her off. "We've been over this before and the answer is still the same." His hands gripped the steering wheel tighter. "The main condition of letting you keep this mare was that you never, *ever* ride her."

Lily slumped back against the seat. She should have known better than to say anything. It was so unfair! He knew how much riding meant to her and her mother. She looked down at her hands and picked at her fingernails. "If Mom had survived the accident, would you have forbidden her to ride, too?"

The silence on the other side of the car was deafening. She'd pushed her father much too far. She glanced at him out of the corner of her eye, trying to see his expression without turning her whole head. *Yep, that's what angry looks like,* she told herself. Coming up was the part where she got grounded for weeks.

Instead, her father gave a long, exasperated sigh. "That will be enough of this conversation, Lily. You know the rules. Please follow them."

Lily let out her own disenchanted huff. It was getting harder and harder to watch her friends ride their horses and be content just to wave at them as they disappeared over the hill. Every Saturday, the kids went for a workout ride with Mr. Henley. They always left the barn laughing and chatting. She wanted to be out there with them, riding with the wind in her hair and the sun on her cheeks.

The first race of the season was only a few weeks away and the others had been working steadily to prepare their horses for the fifty-mile trial. Lily thought back over her father's words. *Could she train Astra for a race without ever actually riding her?* And was the mare even healthy enough now to start? If ponying with Devin and Jericho worked out, that might be a way to get Astra in shape without technically setting foot in her stirrups.

Lily imagined Astra winning a race. She sat up a little straighter on the truck seat. Astra had been in pretty good condition right before she fell ill. Maybe if Lily took things slowly and let the horse set her own pace, the mare would be able to race again someday soon. She deserved the chance to prove herself. Just because Lily couldn't ride was no reason to keep the beautiful Arabian from her destiny.

Twelve

S o," Meloney said, "you're really going to train Astra for the races?" She followed Lily toward the mare's pen.

Lily nodded. "I know it sounds crazy, but Astra seems to be making a comeback. And before she got sick, she was close to being race fit. It shouldn't take that much to get her back into condition again—if she really feels as good as she's been acting." She grabbed Astra's halter off a fence post and went to get the mare. Devin was waiting for them atop Jericho in the paddock.

"But what happens when she's in race shape?" Meloney said, catching up with Lily. "How can you race Astra if your dad won't let you ride?"

Lily stopped and turned. "I'm not sure." She fidgeted with the halter and lead rope. "But Astra acts like she wants to get out there and run. Every time she sees you guys go out for a training ride, she stands at the fence and whinnies and paces the fence like she wants to be there with you. For Astra, and my mom's sake, I've got to at least try. I'll worry about the other stuff when I get there." She continued on to her horse's pen.

Astra lifted her head and nickered when she saw Lily approach.

"Hey, girl." Lily entered the corral and Astra stepped forward, sticking her nose into the halter and lipping Lily's shirt as she fastened the buckle. "You're funny," Lily said, and gently pushed the mare's muzzle away. The gray lifted her tail and arched her elegant neck as they exited the gate, prancing proudly on the way to meet the other horses.

"Easy." Lily pulled on the lead rope, trying to keep Astra under control. She handed the rope off to Devin, hesitating a moment before letting go of the lead. What if the feisty Arabian got away from him and ran off into the mountains, or even worse, injured herself? What if it was too soon to start training like this? Dr. Dale said Astra was fine and could begin more serious exercise. But what if she wasn't up to it after all and the harder work set her back?

"Geez, Lily, you look so worried." Devin pulled Astra into position at his horse's shoulder. "Lighten up. She'll be fine. Meloney and I will take good care of her."

"We'll be back before you know it," Meloney reassured her friend.

Lily patted Astra and stepped back, allowing Devin to swing the horses into a wide circle while he positioned Astra where he wanted her. He stopped to adjust his hold on the lead rope.

"I sure hope she's ready for this," Lily said.

At that moment, Astra snorted and kicked up her heels. The black gelding danced to the side and pulled at the bit.

"Whoa!" Devin laughed as he got both horses under control. "You've got nothing to worry about, Lily. Besides, this is going to be a really easy day for us. We're only doing three miles of easy walk and trot to loosen up our horses. They had a hard workout the other day. Astra will be fine."

Lily sighed. She had to stop worrying so much. The only

way to find out if Astra was in shape was to start training her. She forced a smile. "Have a good ride. I'm going to head over to Whispering Pines and help Thomas and Charlie muck out a few stalls and set up the night feed. I'll see you guys when you get back."

Lily climbed onto the top rail of the fence and watched until her friends disappeared over the ridge. Her shoulders slumped. She felt more alone than she had in a long time. She felt another twinge of jealousy toward Meloney. But Mel was her best friend. She couldn't be mad at her for loving horses.

Maybe someday her dad would stop being so overprotective and stubborn and see how much riding meant to her—and how it was killing her not to be the one to train Astra. Lily pushed the negative thoughts away and focused on getting to work. Climbing down from the fence, she fetched her bike and pedaled to the Henley ranch.

"Hey, Lil-Pill," Charlie called as she came to a stop under the big pine tree near the barn.

Lily rolled her eyes. Charlie definitely needed to get some new material.

"How's Astra?" he asked, following her into the barn.

"Devin and Mel are ponying her out on the trail right now," Lily said. "We're going to start training her to compete pretty soon."

"You're kidding." Charlie's mouth hung open. "My dad might not be too cool with that."

"Why not?" Lily asked, grabbing the red wheelbarrow and searching for a muck rake.

Charlie handed her the extra rake. "If my dad thought Astra would recover enough to race, he'd never have given her to you. He only did that because he felt sorry for you."

Add no tact *to his list of demerits,* Lily thought. "Your dad told me Astra was *my* horse and I could do what I wanted with her. I want to train her to race."

"But you can't ride anyway," Charlie said. "Why bother training her if you can't ride her?" Then he stopped, looking as if he'd suddenly realized something. "You're doing it because of your mom, aren't you?"

Lily shrugged. She wasn't about to go into her personal feelings on horses, or her mother, with this jerk.

"I'll ride her for you, Lily." Charlie said softly.

Lily looked up in surprise. She wasn't so sure she wanted Charlie aboard Astra again, but it was really nice of him to offer. "Really? You would? But what about Derringer? This will be his first big year of racing."

"Well, I wouldn't be able to ride for you all the time, but I might be able to do a race here and there if my dad lets me." He opened the door of the first stall to let Lily in with the wheelbarrow. "Astra has a lot of talent. If she makes it back to racing shape, she can beat Derringer." He grinned. "I like riding winners."

Lily measured Charlie's offer as she forked a load of manure into the wheelbarrow, throwing it with a little more strength than she intended. Part of it fell onto Charlie's shoes. Justice. Here she'd been thinking that he was being nice to her in offering his help, but he just wanted to ride a winning horse. "Thanks, Charlie," she said. "I'll let you know."

She busied herself with her work, mucking stalls for an hour before riding back home to await the arrival of her friends and Astra.

* * *

"There you are." Lily's father came around the corner of the barn. "I should have known I'd find you out here." He looked around. "Where's Astra?"

She pointed toward the hills. "Mel and Devin are ponying her out on the trails." Lily watched her father's jaw tighten.

"Why don't you just keep longeing her in the round pen? Wouldn't it be easier than sending her out on the trails?"

Lily climbed down from the fence. "Astra needs to exercise more so she won't get too hyper, Dad. A few minutes in the round pen isn't good enough anymore. She's used to doing big mileage."

Mr. O'Neil took off his ball cap and adjusted the brim. "Maybe this whole thing isn't such a good idea, Lily. It sounds like Astra is more horse than you can handle. You could get hurt," her father said.

"I won't get hurt, Dad."

"Well, if Astra feels good enough that she needs extra exercise, I'm sure Mr. Henley will take her back," he said. "She'd be home in time to start race season. Isn't the most important thing that Astra feels well enough to race again?"

Lily didn't answer right away, unsure whether to travel down a road she knew would lead to trouble. But if she didn't say anything about her plans to her dad, she'd be in a lot more trouble when he finally found out. "I want to race Astra, Dad." She stopped and waited for his reply. It didn't take long.

"What do you mean, you want to race Astra?" Lily's father practically exploded. "You can't get a horse fit for those grueling races just by ponying them."

Lily knew she was treading on dangerous ground. She wasn't allowed to talk back to her dad, but he was being so unfair! "It was Mom's dream to ride Astra in the Tevis Cup. How can you just forget about that?"

Her father stared off toward the horizon. "I haven't forgotten, Lily."

"Then how can you *ignore* it? How can you forget everything that Mom wanted?" she cried.

Mr. O'Neil's head snapped around. "Do you think I enjoy looking out the window and seeing the reminder of why your mother is not with us anymore? Or watching your face light up every time you talk about horses, and this one in particular? Do you think it's easy knowing that I'm making you so unhappy by not allowing you to ride?" He turned and started back toward the house with long, angry strides. "You're so much like your mother, it scares me," he called over his shoulder.

Lily watched him go, her stomach twisting in knots. It was a no-win situation, she realized. In order for one of them to get his or her wish, the other came up a big loser.

Thirteen

ily shaded her eyes. Three horses were making their way up the trail toward the O'Neils' ranch. From where she stood, it looked as if the exercise had taken some of the edge off Astra's energy.

"Your horse did really well." Devin walked Jericho into the stable yard, followed by Mel leading the gray mare. "She jumped around and played quite a bit on the way out, but once she settled down, Meloney took over for some ponying practice."

Meloney leaned down from Jasper's back and handed Astra's lead rope to Lily. "I'm glad Astra didn't pull much, because my arm is really tired. Ponying is a lot more work than I thought it would be."

"Tell me about it," Devin said. "I had to pony her on the way out when she was full of herself."

"Thanks, guys," Lily said, running her hand over Astra's warm coat. It was early April, still too cold to give the horse a full bath. Astra nuzzled her shoulder. Lily had often seen the mare give the same affectionate gesture to her mother when they came back from a ride. Tears stung the backs of Lily's eyes. She could feel Meloney staring at her.

Devin reined his horse in a half circle. "Okay, I'm heading home. I'll see you guys tomorrow."

Lily and Meloney waved as he rode away. Meloney took off Jasper's bridle and turned the horse into the paddock she'd helped Lily and her dad fix earlier that week. "Are you okay? You're looking pretty bummed."

Lily shrugged. "Yeah. It's just that sometimes I really miss my mom." She tied Astra to the hitching post and picked up the rubber curry brush, working it in circles across the mare's back and over her hindquarters. Astra sighed and cocked a hind leg as she relaxed.

Lily paused with the curry poised over the mare's hip. "If my mom were still alive, I'd probably be riding with you this summer instead of always being stuck here."

Meloney nodded in sympathy. "Yeah, that must be really awful. I feel bad about going without you."

"What's it like out there on the trails?" Lily asked. "I mean…I used to go on rides with my mom, but nothing over a couple of miles. Domino would've laid down and quit if we did." She laughed. "I never really asked my mom about training schedules or anything, and now I wish I had. I'm serious about training Astra to race again. But I don't have any idea how to do it."

Picking up another brush, Meloney started on Astra's other side. "I can tell you what I know. It isn't much, but I've been listening to Mr. Henley." She glanced at Lily over the mare's back. "I bet he'd help you if you asked him."

Lily tossed the rubber curry in the bucket and found a soft brush to finish the job. "No way."

"Why not?" Meloney asked, sounding surprised. "He's one of the best trainers in northern California, and he lives just down the road. You already work for him. I'm sure he'd be happy to talk about training schedules with you."

Lily pursed her lips. "I just don't feel right about asking him."

Meloney finished currying her side of the horse and motioned for Lily to hand her a soft brush. "I still don't get it. I thought you wanted to learn."

"I don't know," Lily said. "I guess I'm afraid."

"Afraid of what?" Meloney stopped her brush mid-stroke. "Mr. Henley? He's harmless."

"I know it's going to be a long haul getting Astra ready," Lily said. "But she's getting better and better. What if I bring her up to race shape and Mr. Henley takes her back? He only gave her to me because he thought she wasn't going to make it."

"But he already told you that he was going to let you keep her."

Lily frowned. "Yeah, but that was when Astra was still really weak. Everyone thought she'd never amount to anything more than a pasture ornament. And my dad would be only too happy to let her go. He's already suggested I give her back."

"Hmm…I see why you're worried," Meloney said. "But hey, that doesn't mean it's going to happen. If it were up to me, I'd ask Mr. Henley for help. But if you want to try to do this yourself, I'll help anyway I can."

Lily smiled at her friend. "Thanks, Mel." The sound of truck tires on gravel caught the girls' attention. Both of them turned to see Dr. Dale pull into the small barnyard. The vet got out of his truck and waved. "Lily, just the person I wanted to see," he said. He handed her a large plastic bag. "Here are some vitamin samples and a couple of containers of supplements. They're close to the expiration date, but still good. I'm sure Astra can use them."

"Thanks, Dr. Dale!" Lily said. She couldn't afford to feed her horse the high-powered, high-priced vitamins they had at the feed stores. The free stuff Dr. Dale had brought would help supplement the meager grain supply she was able to buy.

"Astra's looking good." The vet pulled out his stethoscope and listened to the mare's heart and lungs. "Her heart rate is up a bit," he said, sounding concerned.

"That's because we just finished ponying her out on the trails," Lily said. "Devin and Meloney took her out for an easy three-mile trot and some walking."

"Good." Dr. Dale put his stethoscope away. "You're doing the right thing. Since Astra's feeling better, we should make sure she gets a little more exercise."

"Hey, Lily, I've got an idea." Meloney clapped her hands in excitement. "Maybe you can ask Dr. Dale to write you a program for Astra's training. He's the official vet on a lot of the local rides. I bet he knows what to do."

"A program for what?" the vet asked.

Lily hesitated. "Ask him," Meloney urged. "Or I will."

Dr. Dale looked from one girl to the other. "What's the big secret?"

"I want to train Astra for endurance racing again," Lily said.

Dr. Dale didn't answer right away. *Uh-oh,* Lily thought. *He doesn't think that's a good idea.*

The vet studied Astra for another moment, then nodded. "Sure. I don't see any reason why you can't. Her blood work has been back to normal levels for a month now. As long as you realize that you're going to have to take it easy with her to begin with, she should be okay. Once she gains her strength back, I bet she'll be a competitor to reckon with."

Lily smiled. "Then you'll write me a training program for Astra?"

Dr. Dale put his hands up in surrender. "Wait just a minute there, young lady. I can give you some suggestions to get you started, but Steven Henley is the best trainer in the area. I'm sure he'd be happy to help."

"See, I told you," Meloney said, with a smirk.

Lily gave her friend a light elbow in the ribs, but she knew that she would put it off as long as possible. She didn't want to risk Mr. Henley asking for his horse back.

"I'd keep her with some light ponying if your friends are willing to help," Dr. Dale suggested. "Gradually work her up in miles. Then, when she gets stronger, you'll need to get someone on her so she's used to carrying the weight over those miles." He glanced toward the house. "I don't suppose your dad has had a change of heart?"

Lily shook her head.

"That's too bad," Dr. Dale said. "But maybe someday he'll let you ride. How about *your* training? Are you in pretty good running shape?"

Lily's head snapped up in surprise. "Me?"

Meloney laughed. "Yep. A lot of riders get off and run beside their horses for a while to give them a break. It took me forever to be able to do it without feeling like I was going to keel over. You'd better start getting in shape now."

"Oh," Lily said, feeling a little doubtful. "Right."

"Maybe it would be best if you only ponied Astra every other workout," Dr. Dale said. "Then you could intersperse that with some short jogs with you," Dr. Dale said. "You'll have to build yourself up just like this mare. You need to learn all the ins and outs of endurance racing. Even if your dad won't let you ride, you could still be a good trainer."

"I'll go with you," Meloney volunteered. "It'll be fun. Besides, I could use the extra workouts."

Lily rolled her eyes. "Yeah, it sounds like real fun. Trying to keep up with a four-legged Arabian that's raring to go."

They all had a good laugh. Dr. Dale finished his visit by giving Astra her spring vaccinations and waved good-bye.

"I've got to go, too," Meloney said as she gathered up Jasper's bridle and headed to the paddock. "I'll be over tomorrow after school and we'll get started with our horse jogs."

After her friend had left, Lily fed Astra, then went into the house to wash up for dinner. She couldn't believe that her plans were finally starting to take form.

"Better hurry," her grandmother warned when Lily came into the kitchen. "Dinner's already on the table and your father is ready to eat."

Lily quickly washed her hands and took her seat at the table. "Mmmm, lasagna and garlic bread." She waited until after her father said grace, then dug into the delicious-smelling meal.

"Three pieces of garlic bread? You're eating like a horse," her father teased.

Her grandmother passed the salad, giving her the eye until Lily had sufficient greens on her plate. "You look awfully excited about something," Grams said.

Lily finished chewing a mouthful of the gooey, cheesy lasagna and washed it down with a gulp of milk. "Did Dad tell you that I want to start training Astra to race again?" She waited until her grandmother nodded. "Well, today, Dr. Dale stopped by and gave me some suggestions for the next few weeks of training."

She saw her grandmother glance at her father and guessed that the look on his face was less than pleased. "Oh, I won't be riding her, Grams. Mel and Devin are going to pony her for the longer work, and Mel and I are going to do some jogging with the horses so we can get in shape, too."

"Jogging?" Her grandmother looked confused.

Daniel O'Neil set down his fork, a faraway look in his eyes. "Your mother used to come home from those races so tired. Tired, but happy." He smiled. "The horse would run fifty miles, but sometimes, if she was riding one of the younger horses, she'd end up running about five or six miles beside them."

Lily watched in amazement as the tight lines that wrinkled her father's face seemed to smooth out and relax. Her heart ached for him. It was so easy to get caught up in her own sorrow at having lost her mother that she sometimes forgot how much her father must miss the love of his life.

The lasagna suddenly felt like a brick in her stomach. She reached out and placed her hand over his, trying to comfort him. Suddenly her father snatched his hand from beneath hers and turned a hard glare in her direction, the worry lines back in his face. Lily sucked in a surprised breath.

"Just don't get any ideas about riding that mare once you're out on the trails and out of everyone's sight," her father warned. "I said *no riding*, and I meant it." He tossed his napkin onto the table and pushed back his chair. Without another word, he abruptly stood up and walked away.

Lily traded pained looks with her grandmother while they listened to the sound of her father's angry footsteps echoing down the hall.

"What did I do wrong?" Lily asked, the tears pooling in the corners of her eyes.

"Nothing, dear," her grandmother said. "Your father's just having a very tough time right now. You go right on ahead and train that horse like you planned." She got up from her chair and walked around to Lily's side of the table, enfolding her in a big hug. "Your mother would be very proud of you, Lily. I know how hard this is for you and how much you love that horse. Hopefully, your father will soon come to terms with all this, and quit making both of your lives miserable."

Lily folded her hands in her lap. Her meal was only half finished, but she had no appetite for more. She wanted to believe that her grandma was right about her dad—that someday he'd give permission for her to follow in her mother's footsteps.

But for now, that dream seemed hopeless. She had seen it in his eyes. Her father would never relent.

Fourteen

ily's lungs were on fire and her legs felt as if they weighed a hundred pounds apiece. She leaned her weight into the lead rope, hoping to slow down Astra's trot, but also trying to shift some of the work to the horse so she could have a chance to catch her breath.

"Are you okay?" Meloney looked over her shoulder as she and Jasper pounded down the dirt path ahead of them.

Lily took a big gulp of air so she could get the whole sentence out in one breath. "How far have we gone?"

"About a half mile," Meloney answered.

"You're kidding. That's all?" Lily managed to squeak out between gasps for air. She couldn't believe how easy it seemed for Mel. Her friend was as fleet of foot as her horse.

The green grass waved in the warm breeze and wildflowers dotted the trail. It really was a beautiful landscape, but all Lily could think of was how miserable she felt. Drops of sweat trickled down her back, making her feel as if a spider were sliding down her spine. "I've got to stop," she gasped, hoping her words were loud enough to carry on the wind.

Meloney slowed Jasper to a walk and edged off the trail to make room for Lily and Astra to come abreast. "Wow, you're really sweating. Maybe that's all we should do for today. You don't want to push yourself too hard in the beginning. You might hurt yourself."

Lily handed her rope to Meloney and bent over to place her hands on her knees. She breathed hard, wheezing in and out. Strands of her hair had come loose from her ponytail and they stuck to the sides of her hot, sweaty face. "I can't believe how easy this is for you," Lily huffed. "How long did it take you to get in such good shape?"

"It took a while, and you have to keep it up, or you lose it. But you'll get there, Lily. You're tough." Meloney turned Jasper around, heading back toward their houses. "Come on, start walking," she advised with a chuckle. "If you don't, you might tie up and colic like Astra did."

"Very funny." Lily straightened and followed her friend. "It's really hard running with Astra. I've jogged for PE class at school and it was never this difficult."

Meloney nodded. "Yeah, it can be really hard to learn how to run in stride with your horse. Their legs are longer than ours. You'll both have to find a pace you can live with. Remember, the reason we're getting off their backs and running with them during the race is so they can get a break from carrying us. Slow her down if you need to."

Lily heard hoofbeats behind them and turned to see Devin and Jericho trotting up the trail. *Great,* she thought. *I look like a red-faced blowfish and here comes one of the cutest guys in school.* His timing was perfect.

"Hey, Dev." Meloney waved as he trotted up beside them and pulled Jericho down to a walk.

Lily nodded, afraid of what her voice might sound like if she tried to speak. She felt Devin's stare.

"So, how's the training going, Lily?" Devin asked with a

grin that brought out a dimple in his right cheek.

Lily tried to speak in a normal tone, but she was still nervous around the cute boy. "I'm getting there."

"Great," Devin said. "I'm heading over to the Henleys' place to ride with Charlie and Jill. Our first race is coming up, but I don't think Jericho is ready for it. I'll see you guys at school tomorrow." He looked back over his shoulder. "Keep up the good work, Lily." He winked at her, then squeezed Jericho's sides and trotted down the path ahead of them.

"I think he likes you," Meloney said, lifting her long blonde hair off her neck to catch the breeze.

Lily snorted. "Yeah, I'm sure Devin likes sweaty, smelly girls who can't even make a half-mile run."

Meloney laughed. "I wouldn't bet on that. He's always smiling at you, and he asks questions about you when we're out on our training rides."

"Really?" Lily's heart skipped a beat.

"Really."

Lily stood up a little straighter and matched her walk to Astra's. She'd been thinking that today had been a total waste. But now, it might just be worthwhile.

* * *

Meloney was right about one thing. A couple of weeks after she'd first started jogging with her horse, Lily felt much better. Now she could actually make it a whole mile without stopping to rest—as long as Astra kept her trot slow and Lily leaned on the lead rope to help pull herself along. In another few weeks, she'd be able to make it two miles.

Today she'd put training aside. It was the first race of the season for the Henleys and Meloney, who was riding with her aunt. Devin had decided not to enter Jericho until the next race. He and Lily would be crewing for the five horses and riders in a fifty-mile race in the hills outside of Sacramento. Lily couldn't wait.

She sat in the cab of Mr. Henley's truck, watching the early dawn scenery go by as they made their way to the starting point of the race. She and Devin would be responsible for making sure the horses had food, water, and electrolytes, and that they were cleaned and brushed when they came in from the first thirty-mile loop.

After the horses passed the vet inspection to make sure their heart rates were stable and they were traveling soundly, Lily and Devin would have lunch ready for the riders and care for the horses. They wouldn't have much time before the race would continue, so every minute counted.

Devin, who was riding in the truck and trailer behind them with Meloney and her aunt, had been in multiple races and crewed for several big trainers. He'd already told Lily that their part in the race would consist of short periods of frenzied work followed by long periods of sitting around, waiting for the horses and riders to return. Sometimes the races started in one spot and ended fifty miles later in another spot. In that case, an adult needed to drive the horse trailers down to the next break area. But today's race would begin and end in the same location.

Lily was glad to have Devin there for her first time crewing. Actually, she was happy to be around Devin any time at all.

"Here we are." Mr. Henley pulled into a large field where at least fifty horse trailers were parked.

In the back of the truck, Charlie and Jill had been talking excitedly about the coming race. Now they waved to people they recognized who already had their horses out and saddled.

Others milled around the ride camp, filling water buckets, brushing horses, and adjusting equipment.

Lily felt a surge of anticipation. No wonder her mother was always so excited about the races! The truck came to a stop and she piled out with Charlie and Jill.

"Okay, let's get the horses out." Mr. Henley issued orders while everyone unpacked saddles and bridles and went about brushing horses and putting support wraps on their legs.

Lily finished saddling Mr. Henley's mare, then took a minute to stand back and take in the sights and sounds of race preparation. There was a bit of a nip in the early morning air. They had parked in a flat field next to a stand of large, leafy trees. Contestants who had arrived early parked under them so that their horses would have shade in the later hours of the day when the sun grew warm.

Horses whinnied to each other and pawed anxiously at the ground, ready to be off. People wandered about, making last-minute preparations and packing snacks for themselves and carrots for their horses to eat along the way. Fifty miles was a long way to go, and both horses and riders needed to eat to keep up their strength for the race.

Lily noticed that the dark-haired lady next to them kept looking at her watch and frowning down the road. Beside her stood a beautiful chestnut gelding with two white hind socks and a blaze. Finally, with one last look down the road, the woman shook her head and picked up her brush bucket from the ground.

"Good morning, Sharon," Mr. Henley called to her. "Everything okay?"

Sharon shook her head. "I'm afraid I'm in a bit of a mess this morning. I seem to have forgotten to pack my bridle, and the kid I hired to crew for me hasn't shown up." She laughed ruefully. "Guess maybe I'm just not supposed to race today. Fate seems to be against me, I'm afraid."

Lily felt badly for the woman. She knew how much work it took to get a horse ready for a race. Sharon had to be really disappointed.

"I've got a bridle you can borrow," Mr. Henley offered. "I've been in that position before, so I always pack extra equipment. Here you go." He held out the bridle and the lady accepted it gratefully.

"I guess I can crew for myself," Sharon said. "Taking care of my horse is the most important thing. I can always rest after the race is over and eat my lunch on the trail."

"I'll help," Lily volunteered, looking to Mr. Henley to make sure it was okay. After all, he'd hired her to work for him.

He gave her an approving nod. "That's very nice of you, Lily. You'll be crazy busy, but if you're willing to do it, I'm sure Sharon could really use the help."

"I'll pay you," Sharon insisted.

Lily shook her head. "No, thanks, that's okay. I'm happy to do it. I've heard that I'm going to spend a lot of hours being bored while we're waiting for you guys to come in, so I'm sure I'll be ready to work hard when you get here."

Charlie finished saddling Derringer and mounted up. "Just make sure you've got time to take care of *my* horse," he said. "He hasn't been in very many races and he's going to need some extra attention."

Jill rolled her eyes. "*Your* horse is the reason we're not going very fast today," she reminded him. "Sharon will probably finish in the Top Ten. She'll be in and gone long before we ever get back to camp."

"Okay, then, it's settled." Mr. Henley grabbed Contina's reins and mounted up. "Lily, ask Sharon about what time you can expect her in. You can take care of her, and then prepare for us to arrive about a half hour later."

Lily went to get the details from Sharon while Devin helped the Henleys mount up and adjust equipment. Excitement was high and nerves jangled.

Ten minutes later, everyone cheered and waved as all one hundred horses entered in the race left the starting line to begin their fifty-mile journey. The ride would take them through wooded hills and flat trails across large stretches of wilderness meadow.

They had twelve hours to complete the race to qualify both for awards and credit toward lifetime miles for the American Endurance Ride Conference, of which most of the riders were members.

Some riders would need every minute of the twelve hours to finish. Others would be over the finish line in five hours, or maybe even less. Several horses might be injured or become colicky and wouldn't be able to complete the race. And some horses would take longer than the twelve hours to finish.

Lily watched them go, her heart beating rapidly in her chest. *If only I could be riding Astra and trotting beside Meloney right now,* she thought wistfully. Devin punched her playfully in the arm. "Come on, Lily. We've got work to do."

"Okay." Lily took one last, longing look at the horses as they rode away, then followed Devin back to camp. Someday she'd be right out there with the rest of them. But for now she had a lot to learn about endurance training and racing. When the time came for Astra to race, whether she or one of her friends were riding, she wanted to be prepared.

No matter what, Lily was determined to fight for her mother's dream of making Astra a national champion.

Fifteen

ily woke with a start late that afternoon when the truck and trailer pulled into the Henleys' driveway. The race day had been a big success. Her friends had all finished in the middle of the pack, with a time of just under eight hours. Sharon had placed in the Top Ten.

She climbed out of the truck feeling happy but tired. It took an hour to get all the horses bathed, groomed, and put away. She thanked Mr. Henley for letting her help, then waved good-bye and rode her bike home. It was almost dark.

On the way, Lily thought about Devin. They'd had a good day working and hanging out together. Devin had been a big help explaining what he knew about training his horse, and offering pointers he'd picked up from other successful trainers. He'd offered to ride Astra once a week and pony the mare when he and Meloney rode with the Henleys. Lily knew that was a lot of extra work. She realized that he might not be able to continue if it proved to be too much.

She pulled into her driveway and parked the bike, making a beeline straight for the small pasture to see Astra. The mare lifted her head and whinnied. "Hey, girl." Lily waved a carrot she'd saved from the Henleys' stash. Astra kicked up her heels and raced across the pasture, doing a sliding stop when she neared the fence. The beautiful gray bobbed her head and stretched her lips for the treat.

Lily laughed. "You're such a clown!" Grabbing the bucket brush, she entered the pasture. She gave Astra a good grooming and told her about the day's events. "And tomorrow, I'm going to take you out for a quick jog to warm you up, and then Devin is going to come over and take you for a ride." Astra blew through her lips, covering Lily with horse slobber and pieces of grass.

"Yuck!" Lily said. "This is the thanks I get for trying to make you a champion?" She hugged the mare and climbed back through the fence. She was so tired that she decided to skip dinner and go straight to bed.

* * *

The next morning, Lily woke before the alarm went off. It was Sunday, the day Devin would take Astra for a ride and the real training would begin! She quickly pulled on her jeans and shirt and went to the kitchen to grab a quick bite before heading to the barn.

"Shhhh. Your father is still sleeping," Grams said. "There's a warm cinnamon bun and a glass of orange juice for you on the counter."

Lily raised an eyebrow. "Homemade?"

"But of course!" Grams chuckled. "Only the best for my favorite granddaughter." She kissed Lily on top of the head.

"Grams." Lily feigned an exasperated look. "I'm your *only* granddaughter."

"Ah, but you're still my favorite," Grams said.

"Thanks for breakfast," Lily said between bites of the

gooey treat. She washed her hands and headed for the back door. "Today's a big day for Astra. Devin's coming by to ride her, but first I'm going to take her out for a short jog to warm her up. I'll be back in after they're gone."

Astra greeted Lily as soon as she opened the door to the barn. "Yeah," she teased. "Your feedbag on legs is here to serve you." She put a scoop of grain and some vitamins in a bucket and grabbed a couple of brushes so she could groom the mare while she ate her morning oats.

When she finished brushing Astra, Lily poked around the barn, picking up odds and ends of boards that she and her dad had cut to build the fence. They could use them for firewood next winter. In her efforts to clean up, she came across a blanket-covered pile in the corner. It had been hidden from view by an old stack of leftover boards. The blankets were so dusty and cobwebbed that they blended in with all the other grimy items in the old barn.

Curiosity got the best of her and she lifted a corner of the dirty blanket. *Leather.* Hmmm. Lily lifted the blanket higher and was surprised to see her mother's endurance saddle perched on an old saddle rack. It was covered with dust, but otherwise it seemed to be in the same shape it had been in when her mom last used it.

For a moment, Lily choked up. She lovingly ran her hand across the pommel and stirrup leathers. Her mother had ridden many miles and won a lot of races in this saddle. A tear ran down Lily's cheek and splashed on the saddle, mixing with the dust to create a miniature mud puddle.

She brushed a sleeve across her eyes. Her mom had spent happy times in this saddle. She wouldn't want Lily to cry and be sad over it. Then Lily brightened as another thought occurred to her. This saddle had been used on Astra.

Lily swept away the blanket and pulled the saddle from the rack. A quick dusting was all it needed, and she could put it on Astra to go for their jog. Devin could use it to ride so he wouldn't have to lug his own saddle back and forth. He was doing her a huge favor. She wanted to make things as easy as possible for him.

She carried the saddle to Astra's stall and the mare sniffed it curiously. "Do you recognize this?" She placed the saddle just outside the stall door and went back to look for the saddle pad that went with it. It lay in the corner, along with a bridle, also covered with dust. But a couple of good shakes and a few sneezes later, both items were good to go.

"Here we are." Lily entered the stall and placed the saddle pad high on Astra's withers, pulling it back into place so all the hairs under it ran the same direction. She adjusted the saddle on the mare's back and tightened the girth. Astra flicked her ears and stomped her hoof.

"Hey, lady, don't sass me," Lily scolded as she slowly pulled the girth a little tighter. Next she put on the bridle, then stood back to admire Astra in the newly discovered tack. "Perfect!" she said. "Now let's go for a jog."

Lily led Astra from the barn. The sun shone brightly and warmed her face. The weatherman had predicted temperatures in the high seventies today. In just a little over a month, school would be out. She couldn't wait. Then it would be horses, horses, horses, all hot summer long!

She stopped to check the girth again and figure out a way to keep the stirrups from banging Astra's sides when they jogged. A strangled sound startled her and she whipped around to see what it was.

Lily felt the color drain from her face when she saw her father standing there, his jaw clenched.

"What do you think you're doing?" her father shouted. "I told you that you were forbidden to ride, and you sneak around when you think I'm asleep and do it anyway!"

Lily felt her mouth working, but no sound came out. She wasn't planning to ride Astra! She'd only wanted to use her mother's tack to remember her by, and make things easier for Devin. "D-dad…," she managed to squeak out. "You've got it all wrong."

"Do I?" He stomped forward and snatched the reins from her hands. "It looks to me like you've got a horse ready to ride, and I caught you right before you mounted up." He shook his head, the anger seeming to flow out of him into a pool of misery. "I expected better of you, Lily."

Lily tried to form whole sentences but the words wouldn't comply. "Dad…I…you've got it…wrong!"

"Go to your room," her father said, his voice full of hurt. "You're grounded for two weeks. No horses, no friends. Maybe next time, you'll think twice before you disobey."

Lily stood rooted to the ground, watching her father walk Astra to the barn. She wanted to rail and scream at his retreating back. He didn't understand! He had wrongly accused her. And now she was being punished for no reason. She felt sick to her stomach, like she was going to faint or throw up— maybe both. No horses or friends for two weeks! What would Devin think when he came to ride Astra and she wasn't even allowed to talk to him?

She thought about quickly phoning Meloney, but if her dad came in and caught her on the phone after laying down the law, she'd be grounded for the rest of her life.

It was so unfair!

A loud sob escaped her throat and she tore from the spot, running to the house as fast as her jelly legs would carry her.

She stumbled going up the steps and banged open the door, scaring her grandmother half to death. Lily wanted to apologize, but she was crying so hard, no words would come out. She sprinted down the hallway and slammed the door shut.

Climbing into her bed, she pulled the pillow over her head and let loose with the sobs. She heard the door creak open and her grandmother's soft voice asking what had happened. "Not now, Grams," she sniffed, then felt twice as bad for turning her grandma away. Maybe her father was right. Maybe she was just a rotten person.

Sixteen

ily didn't know how long she lay there, but by the time she stirred it was dark outside and her throat was sore and scratchy. Her eyes felt as if they had cotton stuffed under the lids. A soft knock sounded on the door, and her grandmother pushed it open, letting the hallway light spill into the darkness of the room.

"Lily?" Grams stepped inside carrying a tray with two cups of warm cocoa. It had been a family tradition for years. When one of them was sad, the other brought hot cocoa and a sympathetic ear.

Lily pushed herself up to rest against the headboard and waited for her grandmother to sit on the edge of the bed. "I'm really sorry I yelled at you earlier." She felt miserable all over again, but she didn't have any tears left to cry.

Grams set the cocoa on the nightstand and climbed onto the bed, folding her in a big hug. Lily leaned into it, taking great comfort in the love and support. Her mother used to do this for her. At times like this, she missed her mom more than ever.

"The house is really quiet," Lily said, sniffing. Usually the television was blaring at all times of the day. Her grandmother liked to watch her soap operas during the day, and her dad turned on the sports and news channels at night.

Grams brushed the hair off Lily's face, then reached for one of the steaming mugs, handing it to Lily. "Your father took to the den not long after you went to your room. And he hasn't come out yet."

"Really?" Lily took a sip of the sweet chocolate with marshmallows. It coated her throat and made it feel better. She took another sip, then turned to her grandma. "Grams, I didn't ride Astra, and I wasn't planning to. Dad got it all wrong. He wouldn't even listen to me. It was horrible!"

Grams nodded. "I know, dear, but he knows now. Devin showed up to ride Astra and came to the door looking for you. Your father heard my entire conversation with that young man. That's when he went into the den to be by himself."

Lily blanched. "So Devin knows what happened?"

"No, honey, I told him that you didn't feel well, which was the honest truth. I said I was sure you'd call him later to reschedule."

"Thanks, Grams."

Her grandmother nodded wisely. "There's no reason for him to know your business unless you want him to."

Lily bit her lip. "So why is Dad in his study? I'm the one who's grounded."

"I think he's feeling pretty poorly about what happened," Grams answered. "He needs some quiet time to think things through."

"He's been thinking all day?" Lily said.

Grams nodded. "I'm afraid so. He's got a lot of things on his mind that he needs to sort through." She patted Lily's shoulder. "I have faith in your father. He'll figure this situation out."

Lily hoped she could figure things out, too. There were so many things she wanted to say to him.

Another light tap sounded on the door. Lily looked up, surprised to see her dad standing in the doorway. He looked terrible. His hair stood on end and stubble darkened his chin and cheeks. She briefly wondered about her own appearance and reached up to smooth her hair.

"Can I trade places with you?" he asked his mother.

Grams set her cocoa down and eased off the bed. She gave Lily an I-told-you-so wink on her way out the door.

Her father made his way over and sat on the corner of the bed. He was silent for a while and Lily wondered if he planned to say anything. She opened her mouth to speak, but he raised his finger to his lips in a plea for silence. "I owe you an apology," her father said. "For many things."

Lily raised her brows.

Mr. O'Neil ran a hand through his hair and sighed. "First, I owe you an apology for doubting you today. I now understand that you only saddled Astra for your friend to ride." He paused again, as if trying to gather his thoughts. "But mostly, I apologize for not recognizing how important all of this horse stuff is to you…just like it was for your mother."

Lily sat perfectly still, afraid that if she moved it would break his concentration and he wouldn't finish what he had to say. She knew how difficult this talk must be for him.

"Sometimes I forget that you're not a little girl anymore." He smiled sadly. "In a few more years, you'll be driving a car. You're old enough now to start forming an idea of who you're going to be when you grow up, and to have hopes and dreams for yourself. Your mother would want you to follow those dreams."

He shifted uncomfortably. "This past year has been very

difficult for me. Losing your mother was almost too much to bear. But I knew I had to hang in there for you. I tried to protect you. I couldn't stand the thought of losing you, too. But seeing how unhappy not being able to ride has made you..." He bent forward, his head down.

They sat so long in another space of silence that Lily wondered if perhaps her dad had fallen asleep. Then he leaned forward and kissed her on the forehead.

"Lily, I'm giving you your mother's saddle. She'd want you to start riding again." He rose from the bed and moved to the door. "Starting tomorrow, you can. Maybe you can accomplish that goal of making Astra a national champion and do your mother proud." He turned and left the bedroom.

Lily sat stunned, but only for a second. She bounded off the bed, almost tripping on the tangled sheets. She sprinted down the hallway and caught her father in the living room. She threw her arms around his waist and buried her head in his chest. "Thank you, Daddy, for believing in me. I promise I'll be careful and always wear a riding helmet. I won't take any crazy chances. You'll see. You and Mom are going to be really proud. I'll make Astra the national champion Mom knew she could be!"

Her father hugged her back, then pried her loose and nudged her toward the kitchen. "You haven't eaten all day. Go make yourself a sandwich."

Lily smiled at her dad. "That's just code talk for time to stop all the mushy stuff."

"You're pretty smart, Flower."

They laughed together as Lily made her way to the kitchen to prepare them both a big sandwich.

* * *

This was it. The day she'd been waiting for. It seemed like it had been an eternity. Lily's hands shook when she grasped the reins and inserted her foot into Astra's stirrup.

"Are you sure you want to do this, Flower?" her father asked.

Lily bit her lip and nodded. Her riding helmet slipped forward a bit and she made a note to tighten the strap. Astra turned her head and nudged Lily's elbow with her muzzle as if to say, *Hurry up! We've got lots of miles to cover.*

Lily gave a big hop on one leg, vaulting herself into the saddle. Astra shifted beneath her, wanting to be off, and Lily tightened her grip with her hands and legs. The gray mare sidestepped, unsure of the pressure on her mouth and sides.

"Whoa, girl," Lily said, hearing the quiver in her own voice. Her father reached out to grab Astra's reins, but Lily stayed his hand. She could do this. She took a deep breath and let her mother's words come to her: *A horse can sense when you're nervous. You transmit it through your hands on the reins and your seat in the saddle. You are the leader of this two-horse herd. Be confident, and lead your horse to perform.*

Lily loosened her grip and Astra immediately quieted. Lily smiled at her father. "I'm just going to ride her around the stable area for a bit so we can get used to each other. I want to build a little confidence before I go out on the trail with Meloney tomorrow."

Her father nodded and Lily tried to ignore the worried look on his face as she picked up the reins and guided Astra in a large circle at a walk. The mare moved out smoothly and Lily relaxed in the saddle. She made several circles, then gathered her courage and asked Astra for a trot. After a couple of awkward bounces in the saddle, Lily picked up the rhythm of the gait and posted in time to the hoofbeats.

"Hang on, Flower." Her father swept his hat from his head and twisted it in his hands.

"This is awesome, Dad!" Lily smiled broadly, encouraging her father not to worry. "We're doing great!" She tipped the mare's nose slightly to the inside of the circle and cued her for a canter. "Yes!" she cheered in victory when the beautiful Arabian bowed her neck and moved into the bit, picking up a slow canter.

Lily's father watched her circle the mare several times to the left and a couple more to the right. Then he held up his hand and motioned for her to pull Astra to a halt. "That's about all my poor heart can take today, Lily. Humor your old man, and let's call it good for the day. You'll be out for several hours with your friends tomorrow."

"Sure, Dad." Lily leaned down and patted Astra. She was a bit disappointed that she couldn't stay on longer, but she knew how difficult it was for her father to watch her ride again. She stepped from the saddle and pulled Astra's reins over her head. "You were amazing, girl!" She threw her arms around the mare's neck and hugged her tight. "I'll be in as soon as I get her unsaddled and brushed," Lily told her dad.

She walked Astra to the hitching post and gently removed the bridle from the mare's head, taking care not to let the bit bang Astra's teeth on the way out. She removed the saddle and placed it on the rack in the corner, running her hand lovingly over the expensive English leather. "I did it, Mom," she whispered.

* * *

The next six weeks proved to be very exciting for Lily, but difficult. School was almost out and she had tons of homework to do. With the help of Mr. Henley, Dr. Dale, and all of her friends, she spent four days a week training Astra for her first race of the season—and Lily's first race ever.

It was hard, physical work and sometimes she fell into bed exhausted. But Astra thrived and grew stronger with the new workload. At first, Lily worried that Mr. Henley would ask for his horse back, but after many assurances, Lily finally believed him when he told her the horse was hers forever.

She could still see the worry in her dad's eyes every time she put a saddle on Astra, but he was good to his word.

She spent a lot of time with Meloney and Devin, making training charts for their horses and discussing race strategy. Even Charlie's usual lame comments and teasing couldn't dampen her spirits. She so badly wanted to beat Charlie and Derringer on her first ride.

With Meloney's help, Lily filled out applications for a membership in the American Endurance Ride Conference and an entry into the next endurance race. The fees took a lot of the money Lily had earned cleaning stalls, but it was worth it.

"I can't wait!" Meloney said as they saddled their horses for a fifteen-mile ride in the hills. It was their last long-distance training session before the upcoming race that weekend. "It's going to be so much fun to finally ride a race with you, Lily."

Charlie tossed a horse treat at the girls, barely missing Lily's head. "I'm going to wipe the trail with both of you," he bragged. "I'll beat you by miles."

"Don't be so sure of yourself," Jill said. "Astra's in better condition than Derringer. She's almost as good as Contina. Astra's going to be a tough horse to beat."

"Who's going to be her sponsor, anyway?" Charlie asked. "Dad's mine and Meloney rides with her aunt," he said.

There was silence in the barn as everyone stared at one another.

"Sponsor?" Lily asked. "What's that?"

"Oh, no!" Meloney slapped herself on the forehead. "We were so excited about getting your membership and entry form that we didn't read through all the rules. I didn't even think about you needing a sponsor. How could I miss that? I'm so stupid!"

"I won't argue with you on that." Charlie grinned, then flinched when his sister booted him in the shins.

"Lily, every rider under sixteen is considered a *youth entry* and has to ride the race with a sponsoring adult," Jill explained. "There's only one sponsor per junior rider. I turned sixteen before the start of the season, so I'm able to ride on my own now. We'll have to find somebody to sponsor you."

"And if we don't?" Lily asked, her voice barely above a whisper. Who could she possibly ask to ride with her?

Jill frowned. "We have to. Otherwise you won't be able to ride in the race."

Lily thought she was going to be sick. This couldn't be happening. She'd come so far and cleared so many obstacles. But now, unless she found a sponsor—fast—she'd have to pull out of the race.

Seventeen

Okay, everyone, let's not panic," Mr. Henley said when he heard about Lily's dilemma. "We'll figure this sponsor problem out. Everyone will get to ride in the race."

Charlie finished putting the bridle on Derringer. "It's hard to get a sponsor unless you know someone."

Lily frowned. She knew Charlie didn't intend to sound mean, but still his words bugged her. "Why can't my dad just sponsor me? Or my grandma?"

"Remember, they've got to actually ride the race with you," Jill said. "You have to be within so many feet of your sponsor throughout the race."

Meloney handed Lily some molasses treats for Astra. "Don't worry, we'll find someone. My aunt knows a lot of people. Maybe there's someone she knows who can sponsor you. And Devin's riding with one of the big trainers he used to work for. There might be someone in that group who can help."

Lily finished saddling Contina for Mr. Henley. Astra stood in the cross ties beside her. She had been so excited about the two half sisters getting to compete in a ride together. Now it looked like that might not happen for a while. She gave

Astra one of the treats and stroked her neck. "Don't worry, girl, something's got to work out."

"I think I might have the solution," Mr. Henley said. He'd been very quiet, thinking. "Charlie's fourteen and has over six hundred miles to his credit. As I remember, the rule book states that he's eligible to ride on his own, without a sponsor, if I sign off on it."

"Really?" Charlie asked. "You mean I wouldn't have anyone telling me what to do? How come you didn't tell me that before?"

"You'll still be riding with us, Charlie," Mr. Henley warned. "The practice isn't that common, but it's used under special circumstances. I'd say this is one of them."

Jill smiled sweetly at her brother. "Hey, Charlie, now you'll have to compete under the adult section with me."

"Cool." Charlie grinned.

"Not really," Jill said. "There are more riders to compete against, and it's harder to place."

"Hey, at least I'll beat Lil-Pill and Ssssmelloney."

Mr. Henley unsnapped his horse from the cross ties. "All right, Charlie, that's enough. You keep it up, and you'll find yourself on the crew instead of riding. Then we won't have to worry about having an extra sponsor."

All the girls laughed while Charlie turned red in the face.

"Anyway, as I was saying," Mr. Henley continued, "it looks as if I can sponsor Lily in her first race."

Lily smiled in relief. "That would be awesome! Thanks, Mr. Henley. This really means a lot to me."

Mr. Henley gave her a big smile. "Well, you've earned it, Lily. Now let's get these horses out there and hit the trail. We're only five days from our race."

Lily mounted up and followed the others down the road. She had a tough ride ahead of her today, but it would be nothing compared to the fifty miles she'd be riding this weekend. The race was approaching so quickly, she wondered if she'd have time to prepare for everything. Astra was ready. She knew that much. But she had a lot of doubts about herself.

* * *

Race day finally arrived. When the alarm rang, Lily felt as if she'd barely closed her eyes. She'd been so anxious the night before that she hadn't been able to fall asleep for hours. She just hoped she'd have enough stamina to get through the day.

She rolled out of bed and pulled on a pair of jeans and a T-shirt. Despite the prediction of temperatures in the high eighties, she tied a light long-sleeved shirt around her waist for protection against the sun. Before she left the room, Lily grabbed the photo of her and her mom from the dresser mirror and slipped it into her pocket.

Astra had spent the night at the Henleys' ranch to make it easier to load up and leave early. Lily's saddle, bridle, and helmet were already in the horse trailer. All she had to do was eat breakfast.

She made her way down to the kitchen. Grams had oatmeal and toast ready for her. Lily was too excited to eat, but she knew she had to. It was going to be a long day, with a lot of work. She'd need to keep up her strength.

"Your father and I will be at the finish line to watch you come in," Grams said. "Your dad's going to be on pins and needles, so be extra careful."

"Okay, no handstands in the saddle," Lily promised with a grin.

She ate her breakfast quickly, kissed her grandmother good-bye, and pedaled her bike the short distance to the Henley farm. They were just loading the horses when she arrived. Lily helped get Astra into the trailer, then double-checked to make sure she had all of her equipment and food.

Everyone piled into the truck and fastened their seat belts. It was a thirty-minute drive to the race camp and it passed in a blur as Lily's stomach rumbled from excitement and a bad case of nerves. Would she be able to finish fifty miles? Twenty five miles was the longest she'd ever ridden in one stretch. But Jill had assured her that the extra excitement of race day would carry her over the distance. Lily was glad there would be breaks and rest stops along the way.

"Here we are." Mr. Henley pulled carefully onto the dirt road that led to an open field for parking and setting up their ride camp. "We're running a little behind, so hurry and get your horses ready. We don't want to be late for Lily's first race."

Lily stepped from the truck and helped unload the horses. The excitement she'd felt as part of the crew on the last race was nothing compared to how she felt today. Today she was one of the *riders!*

Astra came out of the trailer and arched her elegant neck, prancing in a circle around Lily.

"Lily, get hold of her," Mr. Henley warned. "Tie her to the trailer before she gets away from you."

Lily followed his advice. The last thing she needed was her horse getting loose and hurting herself before they even started.

Meloney and her aunt pulled into the spot beside them. They had brought Devin and Jericho, too. When everyone had brushed and saddled their horses, Mr. Henley called them over to look at the map of the ride. It showed the basic route, watering stations, and vet checkpoints. The horses would have to pass the vet checks at various places along the fifty-mile route in order to continue the race. Each rider carried his or her own race card where the horse's heart and respiration rates and times on trail were recorded.

Dr. Dale was the head veterinarian at the race and the control judge. If a horse's heartbeat or breathing took too long to come down when checked, or if they were injured during the race, they'd be disqualified. Dr. Dale's word was final.

Lily spotted Sharon, the lady she had crewed for in the previous race. She was parked several trailers down with her chestnut gelding. She waved.

"How nice to see you!" Sharon called. "Good luck today. If you need anything, just let me know. You were such a help to me last ride."

"Thanks," Lily said. "Good luck to you, too. I'll see you on the trail."

"Ten-minute warning!" someone hollered. Lily took several deep breaths, then went to do a last-minute check of her saddle pack, making sure there were plenty of water and energy bars for herself and carrots and treats for Astra. She pulled out the photo of her mom on Astra and kissed it for luck, then tucked it back into her pocket.

"Let's mount up," Mr. Henley said.

Lily gathered Astra's reins and tried to put her foot in the stirrup, but the mare kept turning in circles around her, anxious to be off for the race. "Astra Atomica, hold still!" Lily scolded.

"Here, let me help." Devin took hold of Astra's bridle, forcing her to stand still while Lily made her way onto the saddle.

"Thanks." She tried to smile, but her teeth stuck to her lips.

"Take a big breath," Devin advised. "You're going to do fine. You've been waiting a long time to do this. Relax and enjoy the ride."

"You're right." She took a deep, calming breath and remembered all the hard work she'd done to get to this point. Now it was time to prove herself and Astra.

Trying to get 110 horses safely across the starting line proved to be a bit of a challenge. Everything seemed to be in a state of chaos. Some riders got off and walked until most of the masses had thinned out. Other riders, whose mounts got too excited, ended up being dumped in the dirt before they'd even crossed the starting line.

"Easy, girl," Lily crooned to Astra as they trotted toward the trailhead. She could hear the quiver in her own voice. Her hands were shaking and she couldn't seem to control them. Astra tossed her head, prancing with her feet high and her tail in the air. Mr. Henley reached over and grabbed hold of Astra's bit, keeping her steady as they found their place in the herd of horses and riders.

After about a mile, everyone found their race pace and the crowd thinned out. Lily was finally able to control Astra on her own. The mare still had a full head of steam and wanted to surge ahead, but Lily kept a firm hand on the reins and followed behind Mr. Henley.

The first ten miles of the race passed in a haze as Lily worked to stay focused and keep Astra under control. The problem with Arabians, especially those in good shape, was that it was difficult to wear them down. When the trail was wide, Devin or Meloney rode beside Lily, giving her pointers and helping to keep Astra focused.

Charlie raced past them, grinning, but his father made him get back in line.

"Derringer isn't in good enough shape to be setting the pace," Mr. Henley warned. "You and Jill might have to slow down a bit on the second leg of this race."

"No way," Charlie said. "Derringer's fine. We've got a race to win!" He looked over at Lily and smirked.

Once again, Lily wished she could beat the obnoxious boy. But at this point, her main concern was being able to finish the race and not let anyone down—including her horse.

When they came into the first watering stop, Lily stepped off Astra's back. Her legs were a bit stiff, but she felt pretty good, considering they'd already covered about fifteen miles. Astra showed no sign of being interested in water, despite the rapidly warming day. Instead, she pulled Lily over to the area where several bales of grass hay had been scattered for horses to browse on.

Mr. Henley and Dr. Dale had taught her that horses needed to eat and drink along the way so they'd have enough energy for the long race. During a vet check, a stethoscope was put to a horse's belly to listen for gut sounds that indicated his system was functioning properly. The horse's mucous mebranes were also examined to determine if the animal was well hydrated. If there were any problems, a horse could be pulled from the race.

"Wow, did you see all of that beautiful scenery?" Meloney said. She walked Jasper over to eat beside Astra.

"Scenery?" Lily asked. She'd been concentrating so hard, she'd barely taken her eyes off the horse in front of her.

Devin chuckled. "Lighten up, Lily. Getting to look at the awesome wilderness we pass through is part of the fun. We get to see stuff most people will never get a chance to. Some of these areas aren't open to motorized vehicles."

"Okay, gang, let's go," Mr. Henley ordered. "We've got another twelve miles until we hit our first vet check and required rest."

Astra stood this time while Lily mounted. She settled into the saddle and promised herself that she'd pay more attention to her surroundings on this leg of the route. She urged Astra into a strong trot and found her place in line behind Mr. Henley and in front of Meloney and Jill. Devin and Charlie were the last to mount up. They rode several yards behind the girls and Mr. Henley.

"You tired yet?" Charlie challenged as he cantered past Lily.

She had to pull Astra aside to keep from being bumped.

Then Charlie cut in front of his father's horse, causing Contina to stumble.

"Charlie!" Mr. Henley hollered. Lily gasped as the mare took several bad steps and then righted herself. They all pulled down to a halt while Mr. Henley got off to check his mare.

"I'm sorry, Dad," Charlie said, his face turning red.

Mr. Henley examined Contina's leg. "She's got a small cut on the bulb of her hoof where she grabbed it with a hind foot," he said. "Charlie, get to the back of the line. If you pull a stunt like that again, I'll have you pulled from the race."

Charlie made a face but did as he was told.

"Is Contina going to be okay, Dad?" Jill asked, sounding concerned.

"I think so," her father replied. "I'll need to get a bell boot out of the trailer to protect that hoof when we get back to camp."

They rode for several more miles at a steady trot, heading up into the hills. Lily and Meloney got off and walked their horses up the steep parts, then, still on foot, trotted down the other side of the hill. Lily was breathing hard and sweating in the heat, but she didn't mind. They could go almost as fast running beside their horses downhill as they did while riding them. And the horses got a break from carrying the weight of the rider.

Contina was in such great shape that Mr. Henley remained on her back, but he walked up the hills so they could all stay together.

Half a mile from the vet check, the group came across a small spring that flowed across the path. The clay-based dirt and hoofprints of all the horses that had been there before them made the ground slick. Lily kept a steady hand on the reins while Astra waded through.

Contina hesitated at the water's edge and danced about, trying to turn around. All of the other horses had made it across but her, and that seemed to make Contina more nervous. Mr. Henley steadied her, then gave a small boot in the mare's sides, asking her to cross the stream. Contina danced about again and slipped on the muddy footing, falling forward into the shallow spring. She flailed about for several steps, and then lunged out of the water.

"Whoa!" Mr. Henley cried. Contina snorted and took several faltering steps. The ranch owner got off and checked her. "Great!" he said with a sigh.

"What is it?" Lily asked, getting off Astra and holding onto Contina so that Mr. Henley could examine her more easily.

"She tore that cut on her foot wide open," Mr. Henley said in dismay. "I'm going to have to walk her into the vet check."

Devin and Meloney exchanged glances, then cut their eyes to Lily.

"What does that mean? Why are you looking at me that way?" Lily asked.

Meloney gave her a look full of sympathy. "If Mr. Henley has to pull Contina from the race, then you're done, too. You can't go on without a sponsor."

Lily sucked in her breath. She'd come so far and they were actually well placed in the pack. Mr. Henley had guessed they were only half a mile from the vet check.

While the rest of their group rode on ahead, Lily loosened Astra's cinch and fell into position beside Mr. Henley for the walk in. This would be the longest half mile of the entire race.

Eighteen

Contina was limping badly by the time they made it to the vet check. Dr. Dale rushed up to meet them. "Lily, you can go through the same vet as Charlie." He pointed over his shoulder to the station. "Dr. Atkinson will help you. Have your ride card out and ready for him."

Mr. Henley looked surprised. "Charlie's still here? He and the others rode on ahead of us. He should have been through the vet check fifteen minutes ago."

Dr. Tison shook his head. "Derringer's pulse won't come down. His gut signs and hydration are a little off, but good enough to pass. He just needs to get that pulse down."

"Go on through the check, Lily," Mr. Henley said. "Charlie will help you. We've walked long enough that Astra should go right through now with no trouble."

Lily hesitated.

Dr. Dale looked up from the foot he was inspecting. "What is it, Lily?"

She bit her lip. "Mr. Henley's my sponsor. Everyone says that if he gets pulled, I can't go on."

The vet stood and wiped his hands on his pants, a frown upon his kind face. "That's right, I'm afraid. Unfortunately, there's no way I can pass Contina through this vet check. She might even need stitches. I'm really sorry, Lily. I know how hard you've trained for this race. It's pretty much impossible to find another sponsor in the middle of a ride."

Lily hung her head.

"I really am sorry, Lily." Dr. Dale put a sympathetic hand on her shoulder. "There will be other rides coming up soon. You'll get your chance then. Go ahead and go through the vet check. The experience will be good for you. Besides, you need to become familiar with your horse's vital signs. It will help you with training schedules in the future. And this pull won't count against Astra since it isn't her fault."

Lily smiled her thanks sadly and went to join Charlie. "Sorry to hear about Derringer," she told him. "Hopefully, he'll pass now."

Charlie motioned for her to go ahead of him through the checkpoint. "The others are back at the camp, eating lunch and helping Thomas take care of the horses," he said. "Thomas has Astra's hay net ready for her."

Lily did everything the vet instructed. She held Astra while he checked her pulse and gut sounds. "You did really great today," she whispered to the mare, rubbing Astra's forehead. "You could have stayed with Contina and maybe even have gotten a place if we'd been allowed to continue."

"Trot her up about twenty steps and then back again for me," the vet said.

Lily followed his instructions. When she came back, the man smiled and handed her Astra's card. "Congratulations," he said. "Your horse gets all A's on her ratings."

"Thanks." Lily took the card. It was a bittersweet victory. Astra got excellent marks, which proved that the training program she'd designed had worked and the mare had been ready to race. But now she'd have to wait until the next race before she could try again. And who knew when Contina would be well enough for Mr. Henley to sponsor her again? She turned to Charlie. "Your turn. Good luck. I'll see you back at camp." She turned to leave, but Charlie called her back.

"Hey, Lily… I really am sorry that you don't get to finish the race today. That really stinks."

"Thanks." Lily smiled. Charlie could be an okay guy when he wanted to—which wasn't often.

"It would have been a whole lot of fun to beat you, Lil-Pill," he called after her.

Lily just rolled her eyes and kept walking. She'd changed her mind. Once a jerk, always a jerk. One of these days she'd learn not to fall for Charlie's nice-guy routine. She laughed at herself as she hurried back to camp. By now the others would be finishing lunch or getting ready to head out again.

Race rules stated that everyone had to remain at ride camp for thirty minutes of required rest before continuing.

As Lily entered the camp, the chatter suddenly grew quiet.

"We heard about Contina getting pulled," Meloney said. "I'm really sorry, Lily."

Jill and Devin nodded in agreement.

Lily shrugged. "I'm really bummed, but it's not like it's the last time I'm ever going to get to ride. There will be other races."

Sharon stopped by when she saw Lily tying Astra to the trailer. "How'd your vet check go? We passed ours with no problem. I'm getting ready to head out for the last part of the journey."

"Astra got all A's," Lily said proudly. She didn't feel like talking about it being all for nothing since she wouldn't be able to ride the rest of the race.

"That's great!" Sharon said. "Not only are you a great little rider—and race crew—but it looks like you might be learning a thing or two about training." She looked back toward her trailer. "I sure missed you crewing for me this time. That kid I hired isn't very good."

Thomas stepped up and removed Astra's bridle. "There's plenty more food left," he told Lily.

"I could finish crewing for you," Lily offered.

Sharon frowned. "You can't do that, Lily. You've got a race to ride."

Lily lowered her head and kicked at the dirt beneath her feet. "My sponsor, Mr. Henley, was pulled because Contina got hurt. I can't ride without a sponsor. I'm done for the day."

Sharon stood quietly for a moment or two. She cocked her head as if deep in thought. "You might not be finished yet, Lily. You go get some lunch and get that horse of yours taken care of, and I'll be right back."

Lily watched her walk off toward the vet checkpoint. She talked with Dr. Dale and Mr. Henley for a bit, then returned a few minutes later with a big smile on her face.

"I'm going to be your new sponsor, Lily. I'll be at my trailer. Come get me when you're ready to go out again."

Lily almost dropped her tuna-fish sandwich. "But you're way ahead of me in time!" she protested. "You're supposed to go out now, and I've still got another fifteen minutes left to wait. That'll destroy your chance of placing high."

Sharon chuckled. "I placed well in the last race. My horse doesn't need this race to qualify for anything. It's just a tune-up for the hundred-mile race next month. But this race is important to you, Lily. It's your very first one."

"Oh, thank you, Sharon!" Lily spun around to face her friends. "Did you hear that? I get to finish the ride!"

Meloney and Jill hugged her and Devin slapped her a high five. Charlie just grinned and said, "Good, now I get another shot to beat you to the finish line."

"You wish," Jill taunted her brother. "Derringer had a hard time passing his vet check and you're ten minutes behind Lily in leave time. Astra has a full head of steam and Derringer is tired. Dad is going to be really mad at you if you push him."

Charlie shrugged. "You never know. Derringer is resting now. He might make a great comeback."

Lily quickly finished her lunch while Thomas bathed and resaddled Astra for her. The rest of her group was scheduled to go out seven minutes before her, but Jill decided to wait and ride with her brother. Mr. Henley would be stuck at the ride camp for the next couple of hours, waiting for them to return.

Devin and Meloney finished their lunch and went to bridle their horses. Meloney's aunt was already waiting for her. "See you on the trail," she told Lily.

Lily made a check of her equipment and restocked her saddlebag with carrots and water. Then she mounted up and went to meet Sharon. By the time they reached the checkpoint, it was time for them to start.

Riding with Sharon was quite different than riding with Mr. Henley. She kept up a steady stream of conversation and loved talking race strategy. Lily imagined this was probably the same way her mom had spent the time on rides. Whenever they'd gone out on short jaunts, her mother had talked a lot. The steady hum of Sharon's voice was comforting to her. Lily learned all kinds of cool things from Sharon, like stowing a small cup in your saddlebag so you could scoop water onto your hot, sweaty horse—or yourself—at the watering holes.

"Your horse doesn't like being hot and icky any more than

you do," Sharon said. "If you can keep their temperature down on these hot days, you'll get a better performance out of them."

They did a little cantering over a tree-lined trail where they could stick to the cool shadows. Before long, they closed in on Meloney and her aunt.

"Wow, Lily, you caught up to us so quickly! Devin's probably a couple minutes ahead of us." Sharon began to talk to Meloney's aunt, while Meloney rode her horse next to Lily. The two girls posted in unison. "Astra looks great, but you look like you're getting tired," Meloney said. "Are you okay?"

"I've got to be okay," Lily said. "I can't be tired. Sharon gave up a chance at running a good time so she could sponsor me. And Astra is still going really strong. I owe it to everyone to keep on going. I can crash and sleep for twenty-four hours when this is over."

They stopped at a watering hole and Lily used Sharon's cup to cool Astra off, then doused herself.

"Some riders think it's bad to put cool water on hot muscles," Sharon said. "But my horse seems to enjoy it. I find that he travels a lot faster after that, too."

Lily had to agree that it definitely made her feel refreshed. They let their horses eat a few mouthfuls of hay, gave them some carrots, then mounted up. Lily turned to see if Meloney was ready to go.

Meloney motioned for them to go on. "Jasper's starting to tire and I don't want to push him too hard." When Lily and her sponsor asked the horses for an extended trot, Lily stood in the stirrups instead of posting up and down to the rhythm of the gait. Astra's stride was long. Lily couldn't post properly when the mare hit that big Arabian glide. Lily was just plain getting tired.

It wasn't long before they came abreast of Devin and his sponsor. Sharon knew the sponsor, too. They rode together for a while before Sharon pulled ahead.

"Go get 'em, Lily," Devin said. "You've got a lot of horse left under you."

Lily wiped the sweat off her forehead and reached into her shirt pocket for some lip balm. She could already feel her lips cracking from the hot sun. Devin was right. Astra had a lot a horsepower left. But Lily knew she was just about out of people power. She wondered how anyone was able to make it a hundred miles. How would she ever be able to compete in the Tevis, which covered one hundred miles of the toughest terrain in endurance racing?

Lily concentrated on keeping herself still and balanced in the saddle so she wouldn't be a hindrance to Astra. Her own energy was gone. She just had to hang on and leave it up to the horse to see her through the last ten miles of this race.

They passed several more groups of people and Lily marveled that Astra seemed to be getting better as she went. Of course, they weren't cantering most of the way, breaking speed records like the top finishers would do. But their steady pace kept them moving forward as others tired and dropped back.

About three miles from the finish line, Lily had to get off and run beside Astra. She was tired, but her knees were aching so badly from being bent that she couldn't have ridden another inch.

"Do you want to stop?" Sharon asked. "We can stop and rest if you'd like."

Lily shook her head. "No way!" she said, panting. "I'm going to finish this race." She took off her long-sleeved shirt and tied it around her waist. She couldn't wear that hot thing for one more moment. She didn't care if her arms got burned to a crisp. Reaching out, Lily grabbed a stirrup to pull herself along and asked Astra for a slow trot.

They traveled no more than a half mile before Lily reached the end of her energy. Astra finally began to lag, too. "I don't know if I can make it any further," Lily said. "I'm so tired!"

"Why don't you climb back on your horse and we'll walk for a bit?" Sharon suggested. "Then we can pick up a light trot to finish the race."

That plan sounded good to Lily. She *had* to finish this race. Her dad and grandmother would be waiting for her at the finish line. She couldn't make it forty-eight miles and drop out for the last two.

A group of three riders went cantering past them and Astra came alive, straining at her reins as she tried to go with them. Lily held tight and glanced over her shoulder. Several more people were gaining on them. Her own fighting spirit came alive and she decided to ease up on Astra's reins, encouraging the mare to surge ahead.

"You want to go for it?" Sharon said, her brow raised in challenge.

Lily nodded. "Not so fast that I hurt my horse. But she really wants to go, so maybe we could try a slow canter?"

They rode the last mile at that pace. Lily kept glancing over her shoulder to make sure they maintained their lead over the next set of riders. As they approached the finish line, she could see riders who had already completed the race lining up to encourage those who were coming in.

Lily searched the crowd until she found her dad and grandmother. They were standing next to Mr. Henley, waving and cheering her on. She sat up straighter in the saddle, thinking of her mother as they crossed the finish line. *We did it!* Lily thought, grinning.

She and Sharon pulled their horses to a walk and dismounted to cool them out before going on to the vet check. Lily's dad came running and wrapped her in a big hug. "You did really great today, Flower. Your mother would have been very proud." He turned to Sharon and extended his hand. "I want to thank you for taking such good care of Lily. I hear that without you, she wouldn't have been able to finish the race."

Grams stood in the background, beaming. "I knew you could do it, Lily."

Mr. Henley stepped forward and patted Lily on the back. "You and that mare make quite a team, young lady. I haven't seen very many youth riders come in. You might have placed in this race."

Lily was too tired to do anything more than grin. She wanted to lie down and go to sleep right there. But for the race to be official, Astra needed to pass her last vet check. After a few more minutes of cooling the horses out, Mr. Henley urged them to go through the checkpoint. This time she was in Dr. Dale's line.

"Well, well, what do we have here?" he said when Lily stepped up with her horse. "Looks like we've got ourselves a strong competitor." He lifted Astra's lips and pressed his thumb gently into her gums to see how long it took for the color to come back. He scribbled a few words on her card, then got out his stethoscope to listen to Astra's gut sounds. When he finished, he asked Lily to trot the mare back and forth to check her soundness.

Lily did what the vet asked, then waited anxiously for another minute while he finished filling out her card. If a horse's heart rate didn't come down within a certain amount of time after a race, the horse was disqualified. She couldn't imagine going through everything she'd just done and then having Astra disqualified.

Dr. Dale handed Lily back her card with a wink. It contained all A's and one B. She'd passed with flying colors! She couldn't wait until the rest of her friends got in so she could tell them.

"Oh, and Lily," Dr. Dale said. "You were our third youth rider to finish. You made the top three on your very first outing. It looks like all that hard work paid off. I think your future as an endurance rider looks pretty good."

Lily handed Astra's reins to her dad and ran forward to hug the vet. "I couldn't have done it without you, Dr. Dale. You saved Astra when nobody else thought she had a chance." She turned to Mr. Henley, who had come up behind them. "I've learned so much from you, Mr. Henley. No wonder my mom was such a good rider. Thank you for everything."

Lily and Mr. Henley made their way back to the camp to wait for the rest of their group. After about twenty minutes, Meloney wandered back with her aunt. "Lily!" she shouted. "You were awesome! And Devin placed, too! He's cooling his horse out, but he'll be back in a minute."

Five minutes later, Devin arrived and tied Jericho to the trailer. The horse immediately dug into his hay net. Lily thought Devin looked just as tired as she felt, but he gave her a big grin and a thumbs-up.

"Congrats, Lily!" he said. He walked over and picked her up, swinging her in a circle. "You did it!"

Lily felt her cheeks color. She quickly congratulated Devin on his own success and handed him a carrot. "We *all* did it," she corrected, with a big grin. "I think I'm going to go home and sleep for a week, but I can't wait to do it again."

"Spoken like a true endurance rider," Devin said.

The two of them laughed and talked while they fed treats to their tired mounts and relived the best and worst parts of their rides. Lily felt happier than she had in a long, long time.

Mr. O'Neil pointed to the vet check station. "Here come Charlie and Jill."

Lily, Devin, and Meloney went out to greet the approaching riders. When everyone was together again, Mr. Henley pulled out his camera. "Gather your horses and line up in front of that tree over there," he ordered.

Lily wasn't sure if she could even walk two more steps, but Mr. Henley wanted a picture. She owed him that much for getting her this far.

As they lined up their horses, Lily looked at each one of her friends. She knew she couldn't have made it this far without all of their help—even Charlie's, in spite of all his teasing. Together they made a great team of endurance riders—and friends. She looked forward to racing with them in the future, especially Devin.

Smiling broadly for the camera, Lily threw her arms around Astra's neck and hugged the mare tight. Maybe someday soon, they'd all be posing together as Top Ten winners of the Tevis Cup!

author's note

The Arabian horse is known for its beauty, athleticism, and high spirit. Thousands of years old, the breed is known and owned worldwide. Arabians are smaller horses that average between 14.3 and 15.1 hands high and come in most colors. The Arabian Horse Association, which registers modern-day horses, was founded in 1908. To date, the organization has registered over a million horses and is one of the largest registries in the United States.

The Arabian breed is known as "foundation stock." Many of today's modern breeds, like the Thoroughbred, the quarter horse, and the Percheron draft horse, can trace their ancestries back to the Arabian breed. In ancient times Arabians were used as war horses and mounts for royalty.

Today they are most commonly used as endurance horses that run 50- and 100-mile races. They can also be found in the show ring under both English and Western saddle. Occasionally Arabian horses are raced at the same tracks as Thoroughbreds over the distance of three-quarters of a mile or less. Some people have branched out even further, using Arabians for dressage, western reining events, carriage, and jumping.

For more information check these websites.

The American Endurance Ride Conference
www.aerc.org

Arabian Horse Association
www.arabianhorses.org

about the author

CHRIS PLATT has been riding horses since she was two years old. At the age of sixteen, she earned her first gallop license at a racetrack in Salem, Oregon. Several years later, she became one of the first women jockeys in that state. Chris has also trained Arabian endurance horses and driven draft horses. After earning a journalism degree from the University of Nevada in Reno, she decided to combine her love of horses with her writing. Chris lives in Nevada with her husband, six horses, three cats, a parrot, and a potbellied pig. Her previous books include the award-winning MOON SHADOW, STORM CHASER, WILLOW KING, RACE THE WIND, and many books in the popular THOROUGHBRED series.

MORE HORSE TITLES

by Chris Platt

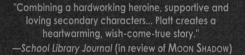

"Combining a hardworking heroine, supportive and loving secondary characters... Platt creates a heartwarming, wish-come-true story."
—*School Library Journal* (in review of MOON SHADOW)

MOON SHADOW
HC: 978-1-56145-382-5 / PB: 978-1-56145-546-1
A young girl's love for a beautiful mustang mare fuels her fierce determination to save the life—against all odds—of the wild horse's orphaned filly.

STORM CHASER HC: 978-1-56145-496-9
Hoping to become a great horse trainer someday like her father and brother, Jessica feels justified in working with the wild Storm Chaser behind her father's back. But after an unexpected disaster at the ranch, going against the rules brings a heavy price...

ASTRA HC: 978-1-56145-541-6
Lily's passion is Arabian horses. Someday she wants to be a great endurance rider like her mother. But a year earlier, when a freak riding accident took her mother's life, Lily's father forbade her to ride ever again. Lily is determined to fulfill her mother's dream. But how will she convince her father to let her ride again?

WILLOW KING PB: 978-1-56145-549-2
Inspired by the true experiences of a real championship racehorse, this moving story celebrates the power of caring and the rewards of hard work.

PEACHTREE PUBLISHERS
www.peachtree-online.com
(800) 241-0113 • (404) 876-8761